CHRISTOPHER ISHERWOOD

Mr Norris Changes Trains

TRIAD
PANTHER

Triad/Panther Books
Granada Publishing Ltd
8 Grafton Street, London W1X 3LA

Published by Triad/Panther Books 1977
Reprinted 1979, 1983, 1984

Triad Paperbacks Ltd is an imprint of
Chatto, Bodley Head & Jonathan Cape Ltd and
Granada Publishing Ltd

First published in Great Britain by
The Hogarth Press Ltd 1935
Copyright © Christopher Isherwood 1935

ISBN 0-586-04794-8

Printed and bound in Great Britain by
Collins, Glasgow

Set in Linotype Plantin

Christopher Isherwood was born in 1904 at High Lane, Cheshire, and educated at Repton School and Corpus Christi College, Cambridge.

His first novel, *All the Conspirators*, was published in 1928. In the following year he went to Berlin and remained there, supporting himself by teaching English, until Hitler came to power in 1933. While Isherwood was in Germany his second novel, *The Memorial*, was published, but it was not until 1935 that the first of the famous 'Berlin' books, *Mr Norris Changes Trains*, appeared, followed in 1937 by the novella *Sally Bowles* and in 1939 by *Goodbye to Berlin*. The late 1930s also saw the fruitful collaboration between Isherwood and the poet W. H. Auden which produced three plays (*The Dog Beneath the Skin*, *Ascent of F6* and *On the Frontier*) and a book based on their trip to China during the Japanese invasion of the country, *Journey to a War*. An autobiographical work, *Lions and Shadows*, was published in 1938.

Early in 1939 Isherwood settled in the USA, where his growing interest in metaphysics and eastern philosophy led to a close association with the Vedanta Society of Los Angeles and to his cooperation on the translations of several Hindu classics, including the *Bhagavad-Gita*. He also worked as a scriptwriter in Hollywood and has taught at various Californian universities. His later work includes several more novels, a book of travel and two further volumes of autobiography.

The fascination of the subject-matter, the qualities of detached humour, irony and unerring observation of human weakness which distinguished the 'Berlin' books were largely responsible for establishing Isherwood's reputation with the general public. The highly successful play *I Am a Camera*, based on *Goodbye to Berlin*, was made into a film in 1955; the musical *Cabaret* became an Oscar-winning film in 1972, starring Liza Minnelli as Sally Bowles and Michael York as 'Herr Issyvoo'.

An American citizen since 1946, Christopher Isherwood lives in Santa Monica, California.

By the same author

Fiction
All the Conspirators
The Memorial
Sally Bowles
Goodbye to Berlin
Prater Violet
The World in the Evening
Down There on a Visit
A Single Man
A Meeting by the River

Collected Fiction
The Berlin of Sally Bowles.

Plays (in collaboration with W. H. Auden)
The Dog Beneath the Skin
Ascent of F6
On the Frontier

Autobiography
Lions and Shadows
Kathleen and Frank
Christopher and His Kind

Travel
Journey to a War (in collaboration with W. H. Auden)
The Condor and the Cows

Translations
The Bhagavad-Gita (with Swami Prabhavananda)
Shankara's Jewel-Crest of Discrimination (with Swami
    Prabhavananda)
How to Know God: The Yoga Aphorisms of Patanjali
    (with Swami Prabhavananda)
Baudelaire's Intimate Journals

Miscellaneous
Exhumations
Ramakrishna and his Disciples
Vedanta for Modern Man
Vedanta for the West

To
W. H. AUDEN

CHAPTER ONE

My first impression was that the stranger's eyes were of an unusually light blue. They met mine for several blank seconds, vacant, unmistakably scared. Startled and innocently naughty, they half reminded me of an incident I couldn't quite place; something which had happened a long time ago, to do with the upper fourth form classroom. They were the eyes of a schoolboy surprised in the act of breaking one of the rules. Not that I had caught him, apparently, at anything except his own thoughts: perhaps he imagined I could read them. At any rate, he seemed not to have heard or seen me cross the compartment from my corner to his own, for he started violently at the sound of my voice; so violently, indeed, that his nervous recoil hit me like repercussion. Instinctively I took a pace backwards.

It was exactly as though we had collided with each other bodily in the street. We were both confused, both ready to be apologetic. Smiling, anxious to reassure him, I repeated my question:

'I wonder, sir, if you could let me have a match?'

Even now, he didn't answer at once. He appeared to be engaged in some sort of rapid mental calculation, while his fingers, nervously active, sketched a number of flurried gestures round his waistcoat. For all they conveyed, he might equally have been going to undress, to draw a revolver, or merely to make sure that I hadn't stolen his money. Then the moment of agitation passed from his gaze like a little cloud, leaving a clear blue sky. At last he had understood what it was that I wanted:

'Yes, yes. Er – certainly. Of course.'

As he spoke he touched his left temple delicately with his finger-tips, coughed and suddenly smiled. His smile had great charm. It disclosed the ugliest teeth I had ever seen. They were like broken rocks.

'Certainly,' he repeated. 'With pleasure.'

Delicately, with finger and thumb, he fished in the waistcoat-pocket of his expensive-looking soft grey suit, extracted a gold spirit-lighter. His hands were white, small and beautifully manicured.

I offered him my cigarettes.

'Er – thank you. Thank you.'

'After you, sir.'

'No, no. Please.'

The tiny flame of the lighter flickered between us, as perishable as the atmosphere which our exaggerated politeness had created. The merest breath would have extinguished the one, the least incautious gesture or word would have destroyed the other. The cigarettes were both lighted now. We sat back in our respective places. The stranger was still doubtful of me. He was wondering whether he hadn't gone too far, delivered himself to a bore or a crook. His timid soul was eager to retire. I, on my side, had nothing to read. I foresaw a journey of utter silence, lasting seven or eight hours. I was determined to talk.

'Do you know what time we arrive at the frontier?'

Looking back on the conversation, this question does not seem to me to have been particularly unusual. It is true that I had no interest in the answer; I wanted merely to ask something which might start us chatting, and which wasn't, at the same time, either inquisitive or impertinent. Its effect on the stranger was remarkable. I had certainly succeeded in arousing his interest. He gave me a long, odd glance, and his features seemed to stiffen a little. It was the glance of a poker-player who guesses suddenly that his opponent holds a straight flush and that he had better be careful. At length he answered, speaking slowly and with caution:

'I'm afraid I couldn't tell you exactly. In about an hour's time, I believe.'

His glance, now vacant for a moment, was clouded again. An unpleasant thought seemed to tease him like a wasp; he moved his head slightly to avoid it. Then he added, with surprising petulance:

'All these frontiers ... such a horrible nuisance.'

I wasn't quite sure how to take this. The thought crossed my mind that he was perhaps some kind of mild internationalist; a member of the League of Nations Union. I ventured encouragingly:

'They ought to be done away with.'

'I quite agree with you. They ought, indeed.'

There was no mistaking his warmth. He had a large blunt fleshy nose and a chin which seemed to have slipped sideways. It was like a broken concertina. When he spoke, it jerked crooked in the most curious fashion and a deep cleft dimple like a wound surprisingly appeared in the side of it. Above his ripe red cheeks, his forehead was sculpturally white, like marble. A queerly cut fringe of dark grey hair lay across it, compact, thick and heavy. After a moment's examination, I realized, with extreme interest, that he was wearing a wig.

'Particularly,' I followed up my success, 'all these red-tape formalities; the passport examination, and so forth.'

But no. This wasn't right. I saw at once from his expression that I'd somehow managed to strike a new, disturbing note. We were speaking similar but distinct languages. This time, however, the stranger's reaction was not mistrust. He asked, with a puzzling air of frankness and unconcealed curiosity:

'Have you ever had trouble here yourself?'

It wasn't so much the question which I found odd, as the tone in which he asked it. I smiled to hide my mystification.

'Oh no. Quite the reverse. Often they don't bother to open anything; and as for your passport, they hardly look at it.'

'I'm so glad to hear you say that.'

He must have seen from my face what I was thinking, for he added hastily: 'It may seem absurd of me, but I do so hate being fussed and bothered.'

'Of course. I quite understand.'

I grinned, for I had just arrived at a satisfactory explanation of his behaviour. The old boy was engaged in a little innocent private smuggling. Probably a piece of silk for his wife or a box of cigars for a friend. And now, of course, he was beginning to feel scared. Certainly he looked prosperous enough

9

to pay any amount of duty. The rich have strange pleasures.

'You haven't crossed this frontier before, then?' I felt kindly and protective and superior. I would cheer him up, and, if things came to the worst, prompt him with some plausible lie to soften the heart of the customs officer.

'Of recent years, no. I usually travel by Belgium. For a variety of reasons. Yes.' Again he looked vague, paused and solemnly scratched his chin. All at once, something seemed to rouse him to awareness of my presence: 'Perhaps, at this stage in the proceedings, I ought to introduce myself. Arthur Norris, Gent. Or shall we say: Of independent means?' He tittered nervously, exclaimed in alarm: 'Don't get up, I beg.'

It was too far to shake hands without moving. We compromised by a polite seated bow from the waist.

'My name's William Bradshaw,' I said.

'Dear me, you're not by any chance one of the Suffolk Bradshaws?'

'I suppose I am. Before the War, we used to live near Ipswich.'

'Did you really, now? Did you indeed? I used at one time to go and stay with a Mrs Hope-Lucas. She had a lovely place near Matlock. She was a Miss Bradshaw before her marriage.'

'Yes, that's right. She was my great-aunt Agnes. She died about seven years ago.'

'Did she? Dear, dear. I'm very sorry to hear that ... Of course, I knew her when I was quite a young man; and she was a middle-aged lady then. I'm speaking now, mind you, of 'ninety-eight.'

All this time I was covertly studying his wig. I had never seen one so cleverly made before. At the back of the skull, where it was brushed in with his own hair, it was wonderfully matched. Only the parting betrayed it at once, and even this would have passed muster at the distance of three or four yards.

'Well, well,' observed Mr Norris. 'Dear me, what a very small place the world is.'

'You never met my mother, I suppose? Or my uncle, the admiral?'

I was quite resigned, now, to playing the relationships game. It was boring but unexacting, and could be continued for hours. Already I saw a whole chain of easy moves ahead of me – uncles, aunts, cousins, their marriages and their properties, death duties, mortgages, sales. Then on to public school and university, comparing notes on food, exchanging anecdotes about masters, famous matches and celebrated rows. I knew the exact tone to adopt.

But, to my surprise, Mr Norris didn't seem to want to play this game, after all. He answered hurriedly:

'I'm afraid not. No. Since the War, I've rather lost touch with my English friends. My affairs have taken me abroad a good deal.'

The word 'abroad' caused both of us naturally to look out of the window. Holland was slipping past our viewpoint with the smooth somnolence of an after-dinner dream: a placid swampy landscape bounded by an electric tram travelling along the wall of a dike.

'Do you know this country well?' I asked. Since I had noticed the wig, I found myself somehow unable to go on calling him sir. And anyhow, if he wore it to make himself look younger, it was both tactless and unkind to insist thus upon the difference between our ages.

'I know Amsterdam pretty well.' Mr Norris rubbed his chin with a nervous, furtive movement. He had a trick of doing this and of opening his mouth in a kind of snarling grimace, quite without ferocity, like an old lion in a cage. 'Pretty well, yes.'

'I should like to go there very much. It must be so quiet and peaceful.'

'On the contrary, I can assure you that it's one of the most dangerous cities in Europe.'

'Indeed?'

'Yes. Deeply attached as I am to Amsterdam, I shall always maintain that it has three fatal drawbacks. In the first place, the stairs are so steep in many of the houses that it requires a professional mountaineer to ascend them without risking heart failure or a broken neck. Secondly, there are the cyclists. They positively overrun the town, and appear to make it a point of honour to ride without the faintest consideration for human life. I had an exceedingly narrow escape only this morning. And, thirdly, there are the canals. In summer, you know ... most insanitary. Oh, most insanitary. I can't tell you what I've suffered. For weeks on end I was never without a sore throat.'

By the time we had reached Bentheim, Mr Norris had delivered a lecture on the disadvantages of most of the chief European cities. I was astonished to find how much he had travelled. He had suffered from rheumatics in Stockholm and draughts in Kaunas; in Riga he had been bored, in Warsaw treated with extreme discourtesy, in Belgrade he had been unable to obtain his favourite brand of tooth-paste. In Rome he had been annoyed by insects, in Madrid by beggars, in Marseilles by taxi-horns. In Bucharest he had had an exceedingly unpleasant experience with a water-closet. Constantinople he had found expensive and lacking in taste. The only two cities of which he greatly approved were Paris and Athens. Athens particularly. Athens was his spiritual home.

By now, the train had stopped. Pale stout men in blue uniforms strolled up and down the platform with that faintly sinister air of leisure which invests the movements of officials at frontier stations. They were not unlike prison warders. It was as if we might none of us be allowed to travel any farther. Far down the corridor of the coach a voice echoed: 'Deutsche Pass-Kontrolle.'

'I think,' said Mr Norris, smiling urbanely at me, 'that one of my pleasantest memories is of the mornings I used to spend pottering about those quaint old streets behind the Temple of Theseus.'

He was extremely nervous. His delicate white hand fiddled incessantly with the signet ring on his little finger; his uneasy blue eyes kept squinting rapid glances into the corridor. His voice rang false; high-pitched in archly forced gaiety, it resembled the voice of a character in a pre-war drawing-room comedy. He spoke so loudly that the people in the next compartment must certainly be able to hear him.

'One comes, quite unexpectedly, upon the most fascinating little corners. A single column standing in the middle of a rubbish-heap ...'

'*Deutsche Pass-Kontrolle*. All passports, please.'

An official had appeared in the doorway of our compartment. His voice made Mr Norris give a slight but visible jump. Anxious to allow him time to pull himself together, I hastily offered my own passport. As I had expected, it was barely glanced at.

'I am travelling to Berlin,' said Mr Norris, handing over his passport with a charming smile; so charming, indeed, that it seemed a little overdone. The official did not react. He merely grunted, turned over the pages with considerable interest, and then, taking the passport out into the corridor, held it up to the light of the window.

'It's a remarkable fact,' said Mr Norris, conversationally, to me, 'that nowhere in classical literature will you find any reference to the Lycabettos Hill.'

I was amazed to see what a state he was in; his fingers twitched and his voice was scarcely under control. There were actually beads of sweat on his alabaster forehead. If this was what he called 'being fussed,' if these were the agonies he suffered whenever he broke a by-law, it was no wonder that his nerves had turned him prematurely bald. He shot an instant's glance of acute misery into the corridor. Another official had arrived. They were examining the passport together, with their backs turned towards us. By what was obviously an heroic effort Mr Norris managed to maintain his chattily informative tone.

'So far as we know, it appears to have been overrun with wolves.'

The other official had got the passport now. He looked as though he were going to take it away with him. His colleague was referring to a small black shiny notebook. Raising his head he asked abruptly:

'You are at present residing at Courbierestrasse 168?'

For a moment I thought Mr Norris was going to faint.

'Er – yes ... I am ...'

Like a bird with a cobra, his eyes were fastened upon his interrogator in helpless fascination. One might have supposed that he expected to be arrested on the spot. Actually, all that happened was that the official made a note in his book, grunted again, and turning on his heel went on to the next compartment. His colleague handed the passport back to Mr Norris and said: 'Thank you, sir,' saluted politely and followed him.

Mr Norris sank back against the hard wooden seat with a deep sigh. For a moment he seemed incapable of speech. Taking out a big white silk handkerchief, he began to dab at his forehead, being careful not to disarrange his wig.

'I wonder if you'd be so very kind as to open the window,' he said at length, in a faint voice. 'It seems to have got dreadfully stuffy in here all of a sudden.'

I hastened to do so.

'Is there anything I can fetch you?' I asked. 'A glass of water?'

He feebly waved the offer aside. 'Most good of you ... No. I shall be all right in a moment. My heart isn't quite what it was.' He sighed: 'I'm getting too old for this sort of thing. All this travelling ... very bad for me.'

'You know, you really shouldn't upset yourself so.' I felt more than ever protective towards him at that moment. This affectionate protectiveness, which he so easily and dangerously inspired in me, was to colour all our future dealings. 'You let yourself be annoyed by trifles.'

'You call that a trifle!' he exclaimed, in rather pathetic protest.

'Of course. It was bound to have been put right in a few minutes, anyhow. The man simply mistook you for somebody else of the same name.'

'You really think so?' He was childishly eager to be reassured.

'What other possible explanation is there?'

Mr Norris didn't seem so certain of this. He said dubiously: 'Well – er – none, I suppose.'

'Besides, it often happens, you know. The most innocent people get mistaken for famous jewel thieves. They undress them and search them all over. Fancy if they'd done that to you!'

'Really!' Mr Norris giggled. 'The mere thought brings a blush to my modest cheek.'

We both laughed. I was glad that I had managed to cheer him up so successfully. But what on earth, I wondered, would happen when the customs examiner arrived? For this, if I was right about the smuggled presents, was the real cause of all his nervousness. If the little misunderstanding about the passport had upset him so much, the customs officer would most certainly give him a heart attack. I wondered if I hadn't better mention this straight out and offer to hide the things in my own suitcase; but he seemed so blissfully unconscious of any approaching trouble that I hadn't the heart to disturb him.

I was quite wrong. The customs examination, when it came, seemed positively to give Mr Norris pleasure. He showed not the slightest signs of uneasiness; nor was anything dutiable discovered in his luggage. In fluent German he laughed and joked with the official over a large bottle of Coty perfume: 'Oh, yes, it's for my personal use, I can assure you. I wouldn't part with it for the world. Do let me give you a drop on your handkerchief. It's so deliciously refreshing.'

At length it was all over. The train clanked slowly forward into Germany. The dining-car attendant came down the corridor, sounding his little gong.

'And now, my dear boy,' said Mr Norris, 'after these alarms and excursions and your most valuable moral support, for which I'm more grateful than I can tell you, I hope you'll do me the honour of being my guest at lunch.'

I thanked him and said that I should be delighted.

When we were seated comfortably in the restaurant-car, Mr Norris ordered a small cognac:

'I have made it a general rule never to drink before meals, but there are times when the occasion seems to demand it.'

The soup was served. He took one spoonful, then called the attendant and addressed him in a tone of mild reproach.

'Surely you'll agree that there's too much onion?' he asked anxiously. 'Will you do me a personal favour? I should like you to taste it for yourself.'

'Yes, sir,' said the attendant, who was extremely busy, and whisked away the plate with faintly insolent deference. Mr Norris was pained.

'Did you see that? He wouldn't taste it. He wouldn't admit there was anything wrong. Dear me, how very obstinate some people are!'

He forgot this little disappointment in human nature within a few moments, however. He had begun to study the wine list with great care.

'Let me see ... Let me see ... Would you be prepared to contemplate a hock? You would? It's a lottery, mind you. On a train one must always be prepared for the worst. I think we'll risk it, shall we?'

The hock arrived and was a success. Mr Norris had not tasted such good hock, he told me, since his lunch with the Swedish Ambassador in Vienna last year. And there were kidneys, his favourite dish. 'Dear me,' he remarked with pleasure, 'I find I've got quite an appetite ... If you want to get kidneys perfectly cooked you should go to Budapest. It was a revelation to me ... I must say these are really delicious, don't you agree? Really quite delicious. At first I thought I tasted that odious red pepper, but it was merely my overwrought imagination.' He called the attendant: 'Will you please give the chef my compliments and say that I should like to congratulate him on a most excellent lunch? Thank you. And now bring me a cigar.' Cigars were brought, sniffed at, weighed between the finger and thumb. Mr Norris finally selected the largest on the tray: 'What, my dear boy, you don't smoke them? Oh, but you should. Well, well, perhaps you have other vices?'

By this time he was in the best of spirits.

'I must say the older I get the more I come to value the little comforts of this life. As a general rule, I make a point of travelling first class. It always pays. One gets treated with so much more consideration. Take today, for instance. If I hadn't been in a third-class compartment, they'd never have dreamed of bothering me. There you have the German official all over. "A race of non-commissioned officers," didn't somebody call them? How very good that is! How true ...'

Mr Norris picked his teeth for a few moments in thoughtful silence.

'My generation was brought up to regard luxury from an æsthetic standpoint. Since the War, people don't seem to feel that any more. Too often they are merely gross. They take their pleasures coarsely, don't you find? At times, one feels guilty, oneself, with so much unemployment and distress everywhere. The conditions in Berlin are very bad. Oh, very bad ... as no doubt you yourself know. In my small way, I do what I can to help, but it's such a drop in the ocean.' Mr Norris sighed and touched his napkin with his lips.

'And here we are, riding in the lap of luxury. The social reformers would condemn us, no doubt. All the same, I suppose if somebody didn't use this dining-car, we should have all these employees on the dole as well ... Dear me, dear me. Things are so very complex, nowadays.'

We parted at the Zoo Station. Mr Norris held my hand for a long time amidst the jostle of arriving passengers.

'*Auf Wiedersehen*, my dear boy. *Auf Wiedersehen.* I won't say good-bye because I hope that we shall be seeing each other in the very near future. Any little discomforts I may have suffered on that odious journey have been amply repaid by the great pleasure of making your acquaintance. And now I wonder if you'd care to have tea with me at my flat one day this week? Shall we make it Saturday? Here's my card. Do please say you'll come.'

I promised that I would.

CHAPTER TWO

Mr Norris had two front doors to his flat. They stood side by side. Both had little round peep-holes in the centre panel and brightly polished knobs and brass nameplates. On the left-hand plate was engraved: *Arthur Norris. Private.* And on the right-hand: *Arthur Norris. Export and Import.*

After a moment's hesitation, I pressed the button of the left-hand bell. The bell was startlingly loud; it must have been clearly audible all over the flat. Nevertheless, nothing happened. No sound came from within. I was just about to ring again when I became aware that an eye was regarding me through the peep-hole in the door. How long it had been there, I didn't know. I felt embarrassed and uncertain whether to stare the eye out of its hole or merely pretend that I hadn't seen it. Ostentatiously, I examined the ceiling, the floor, the walls; then ventured a furtive glance to make sure that it had gone. It hadn't. Vexed, I turned my back on the door altogether. Nearly a minute passed.

When, finally, I did turn round it was because the other door, the Export and Import door, had opened. A young man stood on the threshold.

'Is Mr Norris in?' I asked.

The young man eyed me suspiciously. He had watery light yellow eyes and a blotched complexion the colour of porridge. His head was huge and round, set awkwardly on a short plump body. He wore a smart lounge suit and patent-leather shoes. I didn't like the look of him at all.'

'Have you an appointment?'

'Yes.' My tone was extremely curt.

At once the young man's face curved into oily smiles. 'Oh, it's Mr Bradshaw? One moment, if you please.'

And, to my astonishment, he closed the door in my face, only to reappear an instant later at the left-hand door, standing aside for me to enter the flat. This behaviour seemed all the more extraordinary because, as I noticed immediately I was inside, the Private side of the entrance hall was divided from the Export side only by a thick hanging curtain.

'Mr Norris wishes me to say that he will be with you in one moment,' said the big-headed young man, treading delicately across the thick carpet on the toes of his patent-leather shoes. He spoke very softly, as if he were afraid of being overheard. Opening the door of a large sitting-room, he silently motioned me to take a chair, and withdrew.

Left alone, I looked round me, slightly mystified. Everything was in good taste, the furniture, the carpet, the colour scheme. But the room was curiously without character. It was like a room on the stage or in the window of a high-class furnishing stores; elegant, expensive, discreet. I had expected Mr Norris' background to be altogether more exotic; something Chinese would have suited him, with golden and scarlet dragons.

The young man had left the door ajar. From somewhere just outside I heard him say, presumably into a telephone: 'The gentleman is here, sir.' And now, with even greater distinctness, Mr Norris' voice was audible as he replied, from behind a door in the opposite wall of the sitting-room: 'Oh, is he? Thank you.'

I wanted to laugh. This little comedy was so unnecessary as to seem slightly sinister. A moment later Mr Norris himself came into the room, nervously rubbing his manicured hands together.

'My dear boy, this is indeed an honour! Delighted to welcome you under the shadow of my humble roof-tree.'

He didn't look well, I thought. His face wasn't so rosy today, and there were rings under his eyes. He sat down for a moment in an armchair, but rose again immediately, as if he were not in the mood for sitting still. He must have been wearing a different wig, for the joins in this one showed as plain as murder.

'You'd like to see over the flat, I expect?' he asked, nervously touching his temples with the tips of his fingers.

'I should, very much.' I smiled, puzzled because Mr Norris was obviously in a great hurry about something. With fussy haste, he took me by the elbow, steering me towards the door in the opposite wall, from which he himself had just emerged.

'We'll go this way first, yes.'

But hardly had we taken a couple of steps when there was a sudden outburst of voices from the entrance hall.

'You can't. It's impossible,' came the voice of the young man who had ushered me into the flat. And a strange, loud, angry voice answered: 'That's a dirty lie! I tell you he's here!'

Mr Norris stopped as suddenly as if he'd been shot. 'Oh dear!' he whispered, hardly audible. 'Oh dear!' Stricken with indecision and alarm, he stood still in the middle of the room, as though desperately considering which way to turn. His grip on my arm tightened, either for support or merely to implore me to keep quiet.

'Mr Norris will not be back until late this evening.' The young man's voice was no longer apologetic, but firm. 'It's no good your waiting.'

He seemed to have shifted his position and to be just outside, perhaps barring the way into the sitting-room. And, the next moment, the sitting-room door was quietly shut, with a click of a key being turned. We were locked in.

'He's in there!' shouted the strange voice, loud and menacing. There was a scuffling, followed by a heavy thud, as if the young man had been flung violently against the door. The thud roused Mr Norris to action. With a single, surprisingly agile movement, he dragged me after him into the adjoining room. We stood there together in the doorway, ready, at any moment, for a further retreat. I could hear him panting heavily at my side.

Meanwhile, the stranger was rattling the sitting-room door as if he meant to burst it open: 'You damned swindler!' he shouted, in a terrible voice. 'You wait till I get my hands on you!'

It was all so very extraordinary that I quite forgot to feel frightened, although it might well be supposed that the person on the other side of the door was either raving drunk or insane. I cast a questioning glance at Mr Norris, who whispered reassuringly: 'He'll go away in a minute, I think.' The curious thing was that, although scared, he didn't seem at all surprised by what was taking place. It might have been imagined, from his tone, that he was referring to an unpleasant but frequently recurring natural phenomenon; a violent thunderstorm, for instance. His blue eyes were warily, uneasily alert. His hand rested on the door handle, prepared to slam it shut at an instant's notice.

But Mr Norris had been right. The stranger soon got tired of rattling the sitting-room door. With an explosion of Berlin curses, his voice retreated. A moment later, we heard the outside door of the flat close with a tremendous bang.

Mr Norris drew a long breath of relief. 'I knew it couldn't last long,' he remarked with satisfaction. Abstractedly pulling an envelope out of his pocket, he began fanning himself with it. 'So upsetting,' he murmured. 'Some people seem to be utterly lacking in consideration ... My dear boy, I really must apologize for this disturbance. Quite unforeseen, I assure you.'

I laughed. 'That's all right. It was rather exciting.'

Mr Norris seemed pleased. 'I'm very glad you take it so lightly. It's so rare to find anyone of your age who's free from these ridiculous bourgeois prejudices. I feel that we have a great deal in common.'

'Yes, I think we have,' I said, without, however, being quite clear as to which particular prejudices he found ridiculous or how they applied to the angry visitor.

'In the course of my long and not uneventful life, I can truthfully say that for sheer stupidity and obstructiveness, I have never met anyone to equal the small Berlin tradesman. I'm not speaking, now, mind you, of the larger firms. They're always reasonable: more or less ...'

He was evidently in a confidential mood and might have imparted a good deal of interesting information, had not the sitting-room door now been unlocked and the young man with the large head reappeared on the threshold. The sight of him seemed to disconnect instantly the thread of Mr Norris' ideas. His manner became at once apologetic, apprehensive and vague, as though he and I had been caught doing something socially ridiculous which could only be passed off by an elaborate display of etiquette.

'Allow me to introduce: Herr Schmidt – Mr Bradshaw. Herr Schmidt is my secretary and my right hand. Only, in this case,' Mr Norris tittered nervously, 'I can assure you that the right hand knows perfectly well what the left hand doeth.'

With several small nervous coughs he attempted to translate this joke into German. Herr Schmidt, who clearly didn't understand it, did not even bother to pretend to be amused. He gave me a private smile, however, which invited me to join him in tolerant contemptuous patronage of his employer's attempts at humour. I didn't respond. I had taken a dislike to Schmidt already. He saw this, and, at the moment, I was pleased that he saw it.

'Can I speak to you alone a moment?' he said to Mr Norris, in a tone which was obviously intended to insult me. His tie, collar and lounge suit were as neat as ever. I could see no sign whatever of the violent handling he had apparently just received.

'Yes. Er – yes. Certainly. Of course.' Mr Norris' tone was petulant but meek. 'You'll excuse me, my dear boy, a moment? I hate to keep my guests waiting, but this little matter is rather urgent.'

He hurried across the sitting-room and disappeared through a third door, followed by Schmidt. Schmidt was going to tell him the details of the row, of course. I considered the possibility of eavesdropping, but decided that it would be too risky. Anyhow, I should be able to get it out of Mr Norris one day, when I knew him better. Mr Norris did not give one the impression of being a discreet man.

I looked round me and found that the room in which I had all this time been standing was a bedroom. It was not very large, and the available space was almost entirely occupied by a double bed, a bulky wardrobe and an elaborate dressing-table with a winged mirror, on which were ranged bottles of perfume, lotions, antiseptics, pots of face cream, skin food, powder and ointment enough to stock a chemist's shop. I furtively opened a drawer in the table. I found nothing in it but two lipsticks and an eyebrow pencil. Before I could investigate further, I heard the door into the sitting-room open.

Mr Norris re-entered fussily. 'And now, after this most regrettable interlude, let us continue our personally conducted tour of the royal apartments. Before you, you behold my chaste couch; I had it specially made for me in London. German beds are so ridiculously small, I always think. It's fitted with the best spiral springs. As you observe, I'm conservative enough to keep to my English sheets and blankets. The German feather-bags give me the most horrible nightmares.'

He talked rapidly with a great show of animation, but I saw at once that the conversation with his secretary had depressed him. It seemed more tactful not to refer again to the stranger's visit. Mr Norris evidently wanted the subject to be dropped. Fishing a key out of his waistcoat pocket, he unlocked and threw open the door of the wardrobe.

'I've always made it a rule to have a suit for every day of the week. Perhaps you'll tell me I'm vain, but you'd be surprised if you knew what it has meant to me, at critical moments of my life, to be dressed exactly in accordance with my mood. It gives one such confidence, I think.'

Beyond the bedroom was a dining-room.

'Please admire the chairs,' said Mr Norris, and added – rather strangely as I thought at the time; 'I may tell you that this suite has been valued at four thousand marks.'

From the dining-room, a passage led to the kitchen, where I was introduced to a dour-faced young man who was busy preparing the tea.

'This is Hermann, my major-domo. He shares the distinction, with a Chinese boy I had years ago in Shanghai, of being the best cook I have ever employed.'

'What were you doing in Shanghai?'

Mr Norris looked vague. 'Ah. What is one ever doing anywhere? Fishing in troubled waters, I suppose one might call it. Yes ... I'm speaking now, mind you, of nineteen hundred and three. Things are very different nowadays, I'm told.'

We returned to the sitting-room, followed by Hermann with the tray.

'Well, well,' observed Mr Norris, taking his cup, 'we live in stirring times; tea-stirring times.'

I grinned awkwardly. It was only later, when I knew him better, that I realized that these aged jokes (he had a whole repertoire of them) were not even intended to be laughed at. They belonged merely to certain occasions in the routine of his day. Not to have made one of them would have been like omitting to say a grace.

Having thus performed his ritual, Mr Norris relapsed into silence. He must be worrying about the noisy caller again. As usual, when left to my own devices, I began studying his wig. I must have been staring very rudely, for he looked up suddenly and saw the direction of my gaze. He startled me by asking simply:

'Is it crooked?'

I blushed scarlet. I felt terribly embarrassed.

'Just a tiny bit, perhaps.'

Then I laughed outright. We both laughed. At that moment I could have embraced him. We had referred to the thing at last, and our relief was so great that we were like two people who have just made a mutual declaration of love.

'It wants to go a shade more to the left,' I said, reaching out a helpful hand. 'May I . . .'

But this was going too far. 'My God, no!' cried Mr Norris, drawing back with involuntary dismay. An instant later he was himself again, and smiled ruefully.

'I'm afraid that this is one of those – er – mysteries of the toilet which are best performed in the privacy of the boudoir. I must ask you to excuse me.'

'I'm afraid this one doesn't fit very well,' he continued, returning from his bedroom some minutes later. 'I've never been fond of it. It's only my second best.'

'How many have you got, then?'

'Three altogether.' Mr Norris examined his finger-nails with a modestly proprietary air.

'And how long do they last?'

'A very short time, I'm sorry to say. I'm obliged to get a new one every eighteen months or so, and they're exceedingly expensive.'

'How much, roughly?'

'Between three and four hundred marks.' He was seriously informative. 'The man who makes them for me lives in Köln and I'm obliged to go there myself to get them fitted.'

'How tiresome for you.'

'It is, indeed.'

'Tell me just one more thing. However do you manage to make it stay on?'

'There's a small patch with glue on it.' Mr Norris lowered his voice a little, as though this were the greatest secret of all: 'Just here.'

'And you find that's sufficient?'

'For the ordinary wear and tear of daily life, yes. All the same, I'm bound to admit that there have been various occasions in my chequered career, occasions which I blush to think of, when all has been lost.'

After tea, Mr Norris showed me his study, which lay behind the door on the other side of the sitting-room.

'I've got some very valuable books here,' he told me. 'Some very *amusing* books.' His tone coyly underlined the words. I stooped down to read the titles: *The Girl with the Golden Whip. Miss Smith's Torture-Chamber. Imprisoned at a Girls' School, or The Private Diary of Montague Dawson, Flagellant.* This was my first glimpse of Mr Norris' sexual tastes.

'One day I'll show you some of the other treasures of my collection,' he added archly, 'when I feel I know you well enough.'

He led the way through into a little office. This, I realized, was where the unwelcome visitor must have been waiting at the time of my own arrival. It was strangely bare. There was a chair, a table, a filing cabinet, and, on the wall, a large map of Germany. Schmidt was nowhere to be seen.

'My secretary has gone out,' Mr Norris explained, his uneasy eyes wandering over the walls with a certain distaste, as if this room had unpleasant associations for him. 'He took the typewriter to be cleaned. This was what he wanted to see me about, just now.'

This lie seemed so entirely pointless that I felt rather offended. I didn't expect him to confide in me, yet; but he needn't treat me like an imbecile. I felt absolved from any lingering scruples about asking pointed questions, and said, with frank inquisitiveness:

'What is it, exactly, that you export and import?'

He took it quite calmly. His smile was disingenuous and bland.

'My dear boy, what, in my time, have I *not* exported? I think I may claim to have exported everything which is – er – exportable.'

He pulled out one of the drawers of the filing cabinet with the gesture of a house agent. 'The latest model, you see.'

The drawer was quite empty. 'Tell me one of the things you export,' I insisted, smiling.

Mr Norris appeared to consider.

'Clocks,' he said at length.

'And where do you export them to?'

He rubbed his chin with a nervous, furtive movement. This time, my teasing had succeeded in its object. He was flustered and mildly vexed.

'Really, my dear boy, if you want to go into a lot of technical explanations, you must ask my secretary. I haven't the time to attend to them. I leave all the more – er – sordid details entirely in his hands. Yes ...'

CHAPTER THREE

A few days after Christmas I rang up Arthur (we called each other by our Christian names now) and suggested that we should spend *Silvesterabend* together.

'My dear William, I shall be delighted, of course. Most delighted ... I can imagine no more charming or auspicious company in which to celebrate the birth of this peculiarly ill-omened New Year. I'd ask you to have dinner with me, but unfortunately I have a previous engagement. Now where do you suggest we shall meet?'

'What about the Troika?'

'Very well, my dear boy. I put myself in your hands entirely. I fear I shall feel rather out of place amidst so many young faces. A greybeard with one foot in the tomb ... Somebody say "No, no." Nobody does. How cruel Youth is. Never mind. Such is Life ...'

When once Arthur had started telephoning it was difficult to stop him. I used often to lay the receiver on the table for a few minutes knowing that when I picked it up again he would still be talking away as fast as ever. Today, however, I had a pupil waiting for an English lesson and had to cut him short.

'Very well. In the Troika. At eleven.'

'That will suit me admirably. In the meantime, I shall be careful what I eat, go to bed early and generally prepare myself to enjoy an evening of *Wein, Weib, und Gesang*. More particularly *Wein*. Yes. God bless you, dear boy. Good-bye.'

On New Year's Eve I had supper at home with my land-lady and the other lodgers. I must have been already drunk when I arrived at the Troika, because I remember getting a shock when I looked into the cloakroom mirror and found that I was wearing a false nose. The place was crammed. It was difficult to say who was dancing and who was merely standing up. After hunting about for some time, I came upon Arthur in a corner. He was sitting at a table with another, rather younger gentleman who wore an eyeglass and had sleek dark hair.

'Ah, here you are, William. We were beginning to fear that you'd deserted us. May I introduce two of my most valued friends to each other? Mr Bradshaw – Baron von Pregnitz.'

The Baron, who was fishy and suave, inclined his head. Leaning towards me, like a cod swimming up through water, he asked:

'Excuse me. Do you know Naples?'

'No. I've never been there.'

'Forgive me. I'm sorry. I had the feeling that we'd met each other before.'

'Perhaps so,' I said politely, wondering how he could smile without dropping his eyeglass. It was rimless and ribbonless and looked as though it had been screwed into his pink well-shaved face by means of some horrible surgical operation.

'Perhaps you were at Juan-les-Pins last year?'

'No, I'm afraid I wasn't.'

'Yes, I see.' He smiled in polite regret. 'In that case I must beg your pardon.'

'Don't mention it,' I said. We both laughed very heartily. Arthur, evidently pleased that I was making a good impression on the Baron, laughed too. I drank a glass of champagne off at a gulp. A three-man band was playing: *Gruss' mir mein Hawai, ich bleib' Dir treu, ich hab' Dich gerne*. The dancers, locked frigidly together, swayed in partial-paralytic rhythms under a huge sunshade suspended from the ceiling and oscillating gently through cigarette smoke and hot rising air.

'Don't you find it a trifle stuffy in here?' Arthur asked anxiously.

In the windows were bottles filled with coloured liquids brilliantly illuminated from beneath, magenta, emerald, vermilion. They seemed to be lighting up the whole room. The cigarette smoke made my eyes smart until the tears ran down my face. The music kept dying away, then surging up fearfully loud. I passed my hand down the shiny black oilcloth curtains in the alcove behind my chair. Oddly enough, they were quite cold. The lamps were like alpine cowbells. And there was a fluffy white monkey perched above the bar. In another moment, when I had drunk exactly the right amount of champagne, I should have a vision. I took a sip. And now, with extreme clarity, without passion or malice, I saw what Life really is. It had something, I remember, to do with the revolving sunshade. Yes, I murmured to myself, let them dance. They are dancing. I am glad.

'You know, I like this place. Extraordinarily,' I told the Baron with enthusiasm. He did not seem surprised.

Arthur was solemnly stifling a belch.

'Dear Arthur, don't look so sad. Are you tired?'

'No, not tired, William. Only a little contemplative, perhaps. Such an occasion as this is not without its solemn aspect. You young people are quite right to enjoy yourselves. I don't blame you for a moment. One has one's memories.'

'Memories are the most precious things we have,' said the Baron with approval. As intoxication proceeded, his face seemed slowly to disintegrate. A rigid area of paralysis formed round the monocle. The monocle was holding his face together. He gripped it desperately with his facial muscles, cocking his disengaged eyebrow, his mouth sagging slightly at the corners, minute beads of perspiration appearing along the parting of his thin, satin-smooth dark hair. Catching my eye, he swam up towards me, to the surface of the element which seemed to separate us.

'Excuse me, please. May I ask you something?'

'By all means.'

'Have you read *Winnie the Pooh*, by A. A. Milne?'

'Yes, I have.'

'And tell me, please, how did you like it?'

'Very much indeed.'

'Then I am very glad. Yes, so did I. Very much.'

And now we were all standing up. What had happened? It was midnight. Our glasses touched.

'Cheerio,' said the Baron, with the air of one who makes a particularly felicitous quotation.

'Allow me,' said Arthur, 'to wish you both every success

and happiness in nineteen thirty-one. Every success ...' His voice trailed off uneasily into silence. Nervously he fingered his heavy fringe of hair. A tremendous crash exploded from the band. Like a car which has slowly, laboriously reached the summit of the mountain railway, we plunged headlong downwards into the New Year.

The events of the next two hours were somewhat confused. We were in a small bar, where I remember only the ruffled plumes of a paper streamer, crimson, very beautiful, stirring like seaweed in the draught from an electric fan. We wandered through streets crowded with girls who popped teasers in our faces. We ate ham and eggs in the first-class restaurant of the Friedrichstrasse Station. Arthur had disappeared. The Baron was rather mysterious and sly about this; though I couldn't understand why. He had asked me to call him Kuno, and explained how much he admired the character of the English upper class. We were driving in a taxi, alone. The Baron told me about a friend of his, a young Etonian. The Etonian had been in India for two years. On the morning after his return, he had met his oldest school-friend in Bond Street. Although they hadn't seen each other for so long, the school-friend had merely said: 'Hullo. I'm afraid I can't talk to you now. I have to go shopping with my mother.' 'And I find this so very nice,' the Baron concluded. 'It is your English self-control, you see.' The taxi crossed several bridges and passed a gas-works. The Baron pressed my hand and made me a long speech about how wonderful it is to be young. He had become rather indistinct and his English was rapidly deteriorating. 'You see, excuse me, I've been watching your reactions the whole evening. I hope you are not offended?' I found my false nose in my pocket and put it on. It had got a bit crumpled. The Baron seemed impressed. 'This is all so very interesting for me, you see.' Soon after this, I had to stop the taxi under a lamp-post in order to be sick.

We were driving along a street bounded by a high dark wall. Over the top of the wall I suddenly caught sight of an ornamental cross. 'Good God,' I said. 'Are you taking me to the cemetery?'

The Baron merely smiled. We had stopped; having arrived, it seemed, at the blackest corner of the night. I stumbled over something and the Baron obligingly took my arm. He seemed to have been here before. We passed through an archway and into a courtyard. There was light here from several windows, and snatches of gramophone music and laughter. A silhouetted head and shoulders leant out of one of the windows, shouted: *'Prosit Neujahr!'* and spat vigorously. The spittle landed with a soft splash on the paving-stone just beside my foot. Other heads emerged from other windows. 'Is that you, Paul, you sow?' someone shouted. 'Red Front!' yelled a voice, and a louder splash followed. This time, I think, a beer-mug had been emptied.

Here one of the anæsthetic periods of my evening supervened. How the Baron got me upstairs, I don't know. It was quite painless. We were in a room full of people dancing, shouting, singing, drinking, shaking our hands and thumping us on the back. There was an immense ornamental gasolier, converted to hold electric bulbs and enmeshed in paper festoons. My glance reeled about the room, picking out large or minute objects, a bowl of claret-cup in which floated an empty match-box, a broken bead from a necklace, a bust of Bismarck on the top of a Gothic dresser – holding them for an instant, then losing them again in general coloured chaos. In this manner, I caught a sudden startling glimpse of Arthur's head, its mouth open, the wig jammed down over its left eye. I stumbled about looking for the body and collapsed comfortably on to a sofa, holding the upper half of a girl. My face was buried in dusty-smelling lace cushions. The noise of the party burst over me in thundering waves, like the sea. It was strangely soothing. 'Don't go to sleep, darling,' said the girl I was holding. 'No, of course I won't,' I replied, and sat up, tidying my hair. I felt suddenly quite sober.

Opposite me, in a big armchair, sat Arthur, with a thin, dark, sulky-looking girl on his lap. He had taken off his coat and waistcoat and looked most domestic. He wore gaudily striped braces. His shirt-sleeves were looped up with elastic bands. Except for a little hair round the base of the skull, he was perfectly bald.

'What on earth have you done with it?' I exclaimed. 'You'll catch cold.'

'The idea was not mine, William. Rather a graceful tribute, don't you think, to the Iron Chancellor?'

He seemed in much better spirits, now, than earlier in the evening, and, strangely enough, not at all drunk. He had a remarkably strong head. Looking up, I saw the wig perched rakishly on Bismarck's helmet. It was much too big for him.

Turning, I found the Baron sitting beside me on the sofa. 'Hullo, Kuno,' I said. 'How did you get here?'

He didn't answer, but smiled his bright rigid smile and desperately cocked an eyebrow. He seemed on the very point of collapse. In another moment, his monocle would fall out.

The gramophone burst into loud braying music. Most of the people in the room began to dance. They were nearly all young. The boys were in shirt-sleeves; the girls had un-hooked their dresses. The atmosphere of the room was heavy with dust and perspiration and cheap scent. An enormous woman elbowed her way through the crowd, carrying a glass of wine in each hand. She wore a pink silk blouse and a very short pleated white skirt; her feet were jammed into absurdly small high-heeled shoes, out of which bulged pads of silk-stockinged flesh. Her cheeks were waxy pink and her hair dyed tinsel-golden, so that it matched the glitter of the half-dozen bracelets on her powdered arms. She was as curious and sinister as a life-size doll. Like a doll, she had staring china-blue eyes which did not laugh, although her lips were parted in a smile revealing several gold teeth.

'This is Olga, our hostess,' Arthur explained.

'Hullo, Baby!' Olga handed me a glass. She pinched Arthur's cheek: 'Well, my little turtle-dove?'

The gesture was so perfunctory that it reminded me of a vet with a horse. Arthur giggled: 'Hardly what one would call a strikingly well-chosen epithet, is it? A turtle-dove. What do you say to that, Anni?' He addressed the dark girl on his knee. 'You're very silent, you know. You don't sparkle this evening. Or does the presence of the extremely handsome young man opposite distract your thoughts? William, I believe you've made a conquest. I do indeed.'

32

Anni smiled at this, a slight self-possessed whore's smile. Then she scratched her thigh, and yawned. She wore a smartly cut little black jacket and a black skirt. On her legs were a pair of long black boots, laced up to the knee. They had a curious design in gold running round the tops. They gave to her whole costume the effect of a kind of uniform.

'Ah, you're admiring Anni's boots,' said Arthur, with satisfaction. 'But you ought to see her other pair. Scarlet leather with black heels. I had them made for her myself. Anni won't wear them in the street; she says they make her look too conspicuous. But sometimes, if she's feeling particularly *energetic*, she puts them on when she comes to see me.'

Meanwhile, several of the girls and boys had stopped dancing. They stood round us, their arms interlaced, their eyes fixed on Arthur's mouth with the naïve interest of savages, as though they expected to see the words jump visibly out of his throat. One of the boys began to laugh. 'Oh yes,' he mimicked. 'I spik you Englisch, no?'

Arthur's hand was straying abstractedly over Anni's thigh. She raised herself and smacked it sharply, with the impersonal viciousness of a cat.

'Oh dear, I'm afraid you're in a very *cruel* mood, this evening! I see I shall be *corrected* for this. Anni is an exceedingly severe young lady.' Arthur sniggered loudly; continued conversationally in English: 'Don't you think it's an exquisitely beautiful face? Quite perfect, in its way. Like a Raphael Madonna. The other day I made an epigram. I said, Anni's beauty is only *sin*-deep. I hope that's original? Is it? Please laugh.'

'I think it's very good indeed.'

'Only *sin*-deep. I'm glad you like it. My first thought was, I must tell that to William. You positively inspire me, you know. You make me sparkle. I always say that I only wish to have three sorts of people as my friends, those who are very rich, those who are very witty, and those who are very beautiful. You, my dear William, belong to the second category.'

I could guess to which category Baron von Pregnitz belonged, and looked round to see whether he had been listening. But the Baron was otherwise engaged. He reclined upon the farther end of the sofa in the embrace of a powerful youth in a boxer's sweater, who was gradually forcing a mugful of beer down his throat. The Baron protested feebly; the beer was spilling all over him.

I became aware that I had my arm round a girl. Perhaps she had been there all the time. She snuggled against me, while from the other side a boy was amateurishly trying to pick my pocket. I opened my mouth to protest, but thought better of it. Why make a scene at the end of such an enjoyable evening? He was welcome to my money. I only had three marks left at the most. The Baron would pay for everything, anyhow. At that moment, I saw his face with almost microscopic distinctness. He had, as I noticed now for the first time, been taking artificial sunlight treatment. The skin round his nose was just beginning to peel. How nice he was! I raised my glass to him. His fish-eye gleamed faintly over the boxer's arm and he made a slight movement of his head. He was beyond speech. When I turned round, Arthur and Anni had disappeared.

With the vague intention of going to look for them, I staggered to my feet, only to become involved in the dancing, which had broken out again with renewed vigour. I was seized round the waist, round the neck, kissed, hugged, tickled, half undressed; I danced with girls, with boys, with two or three people at the same time. It may have been five or ten minutes before I reached the door at the farther end of the room. Beyond the door was a pitch-dark passage with a crack of light at the end of it. The passage was crammed so full of furniture that one could only edge one's way along it sideways. I had wriggled and shuffled about half the distance, when an agonized cry came from the lighted room ahead of me.

'*Nein, nein!* Mercy! oh dear! *Hilfe! Hilfe!*'

There was no mistaking the voice. They had got Arthur in there, and were robbing him and knocking him about. I might have known it. We were fools ever to have poked our noses into a place like this. We had only ourselves to thank.

Drink made me brave. Struggling forward to the door, I pushed it open.

The first person I saw was Anni. She was standing in the middle of the room. Arthur cringed on the floor at her feet. He had removed several more of his garments, and was now dressed, lightly but with perfect decency, in a suit of mauve silk underwear, a rubber abdominal belt and a pair of socks. In one hand he held a brush and in the other a yellow shoe-rag. Olga towered behind him, brandishing a heavy leather whip.

'You call that clean, you swine!' she cried, in a terrible voice. 'Do them again this minute! And if I find a speck of dirt on them I'll thrash you till you can't sit down for a week.'

As she spoke she gave Arthur a smart cut across the buttocks. He uttered a squeal of pain and pleasure, and began to brush and polish Anni's boots with feverish haste.

'Mercy! Mercy!' Arthur's voice was shrill and gleeful, like a child's when it is shamming. 'Stop! You're killing me!'

'Killing's too good for you,' retorted Olga, administering another cut. 'I'll skin you alive!'

'Oh! Oh! Stop! Mercy! Oh!'

They were making such a noise that they hadn't heard me bang open the door. Now they saw me, however. My presence did not seem to disconcert any of them in the least. Indeed, it appeared to add spice to Arthur's enjoyment.

'Oh dear! William, save me! You won't? You're as cruel as the rest of them. Anni, my love! Olga! Just look how she treats me. Goodness knows what they won't be making me do in a minute!'

'Come in, Baby,' cried Olga, with tigerish jocularity. 'Just you wait! It's your turn next. I'll make you cry for Mummy!'

She made a playful slash at me with the whip which sent me in headlong retreat down the passage, pursued by Arthur's delighted and anguished cries.

Several hours later I woke to find myself lying curled up on the floor, with my face pressed against the leg of the sofa. I had a head like a furnace, and pains in every bone. The party was over. Half a dozen people lay insensible about the dismantled room, sprawling in various attitudes of extreme discomfort. Daylight gleamed through the slats of the venetian blinds.

After making sure that neither Arthur nor the Baron were among the fallen, I picked my way over their bodies, out of the flat, downstairs, across the courtyard and into the street. The whole building seemed to be full of dead drunks. I met nobody.

I found myself in one of the back streets near the canal, not far from the Möckernbrücke Station, about half an hour from my lodgings. I had no money for the electric train. And, anyhow, a walk would do me good. I limped home, along dreary streets where paper streamers hung from the sills of damp, blank houses, or were entangled in the clammy twigs of the trees. When I arrived, my landlady greeted me with the news that Arthur had rung up already three times to know how I was.

'Such a nice-spoken gentleman, I always think. And so considerate.'

I agreed with her, and went to bed.

CHAPTER FOUR

Frl. Schroeder, my landlady, was very fond of Arthur. Over the telephone, she always addressed him as *Herr Doktor*, her highest mark of esteem.

'Ah, is that you, *Herr Doktor*? But of course I recognize your voice; I should know it in a million. You sound very tired this morning. Another of your late nights? *Na, na,* you can't expect an old woman like me to believe that; I know what gentlemen are when they go out on the spree ... What's that you say? Stuff and nonsense! You flatterer! Well, well, you men are all alike; from seventeen to seventy ... *Pfui!* I'm surprised at you ... No, I most certainly shall not! Ha, ha! You want to speak to Herr Bradshaw? Why, of course, I'd quite forgotten. I'll call him at once.'

When Arthur came to tea with me, Frl. Schroeder would put on her black velvet dress, which was cut low at the neck, and her string of Woolworth pearls. With her cheeks rouged and her eyelids darkened, she would open the door to him, looking like a caricature of Mary, Queen of Scots. I remarked on this to Arthur, who was delighted.

'Really, William, you're most unkind. You say such sharp things. I'm beginning to be afraid of your tongue, I am indeed.'

After this he usually referred to Frl. Schroeder as Her Majesty. *La divine* Schroeder was another favourite epithet.

No matter how much of a hurry he was in, he always found time for a few minutes' flirtation with her, brought her flowers, sweets, cigarettes, and sympathized with every fluctuation in the delicate health of Hanns, her canary. When Hanns finally died and Frl. Schroeder shed tears, I thought Arthur was going to cry too. He was genuinely upset. 'Dear, dear,' he kept repeating. 'Nature is really very cruel.'

My other friends were less enthusiastic about Arthur. I introduced him to Helen Pratt, but the meeting was not a success. At that time Helen was Berlin correspondent to one of the London political weeklies, and supplemented her income by making translations and giving English lessons. We sometimes passed on pupils to each other. She was a pretty, fair-haired, fragile-looking girl, hard as nails, who had been educated at the University of London and took Sex seriously. She was accustomed to spending her days and nights in male society and had little use for the company of other girls. She could drink most of the English journalists under the table, and sometimes did so, but more as a matter of principle than because she enjoyed it. The first time she met you, she called you by your Christian name and informed you that her parents kept a tobacco and sweet shop in Shepherd's Bush. This was her method of 'testing' character; your reaction to the news damned or saved you finally in her estimation. Above all else, Helen loathed being reminded that she was a woman; except in bed.

Arthur, as I saw too late, had no technique whatsoever for dealing with her sort. From the first moment he was frankly scared of her. She brushed aside all the little polished politenesses which shielded his timid soul. 'Hullo, you two,' she said, casually reaching out a hand over the newspaper she was reading. (We had met by appointment in a small restaurant behind the Memorial Church.)

Arthur gingerly took the hand she offered. He lingered uneasily beside the table, fidgeted, awaiting the ritual to which he was accustomed. Nothing happened. He cleared his throat, coughed:

'Will you allow me to take a seat?'

Helen, who was about to read something aloud from the newspaper, glanced up at him as though she'd forgotten his existence and was surprised to find him still there.

'What's the matter?' she asked. 'Aren't there enough chairs?'

We got talking, somehow, about Berlin night life. Arthur giggled and became arch. Helen, who dealt in statistics and psycho-analytical terms, regarded him in puzzled disapproval. At length Arthur made a sly reference to 'the speciality of the Kaufhaus des Westens.'

'Oh, you mean those whores on the corner there,' said Helen, in the bright matter-of-fact tone of a schoolmistress giving a biology lesson, 'who dress up to excite the boot-fetishists?'

'Well, upon my soul, ha ha, I must say,' Arthur sniggered, coughed and rapidly fingered his wig, 'seldom have I met such an extremely, if you'll allow me to say so, er – *advanced*, or shall I say, er – *modern* young lady . . .'

'My God!' Helen threw back her head and laughed unpleasantly. 'I haven't been called a young lady since the days when I used to help mother with the shop on Saturday afternoons.'

'Have you – er – been in this city long?' asked Arthur hastily. Vaguely aware that he had made a mistake, he imagined that he ought to change the subject. I saw the look Helen gave him and knew that all was over.

'If you take my advice, Bill,' she said to me, the next time we met, 'you won't trust that man an inch.'

'I don't,' I said.

'Oh, I know you. You're soft, like most men. You make up romances about people instead of seeing them as they are. Have you ever noticed his mouth?'

'Frequently.'

'Ugh, it's disgusting. I could hardly bear to look at it. Beastly and flabby like a toad's.'

'Well,' I said, laughing, 'I suppose I've got a weakness for toads.'

Not daunted by this failure, I tried Arthur on Fritz Wendel. Fritz was a German-American, a young man about town, who spent his leisure time dancing and playing bridge. He had a curious passion for the society of painters and writers, and had acquired a status with them by working at a fashionable art dealer's. The art dealer didn't pay him anything, but Fritz could afford this hobby, being rich. He had an aptitude for gossip which amounted to talent, and might have made a first-class private detective.

We had tea together in Fritz's flat. He and Arthur talked New York, impressionist painting, and the unpublished works of the Wilde group. Arthur was witty and astonishingly informative. Fritz's black eyes sparkled as he registered the epigrams for future use, and I smiled, feeling pleased and proud. I felt myself personally responsible for the success of the interview. I was childishly anxious that Arthur should be approved of; perhaps because I, too, wanted to be finally, completely convinced.

We said good-bye with mutual promises of an early future meeting. A day or two later, I happened to see Fritz in the street. From the pleasure with which he greeted me, I knew at once that he had something extra spiteful to tell me. For a quarter of an hour he chatted gaily about bridge, night clubs, and his latest flame, a well-known sculptress; his malicious smile broadening all the while at the thought of the tit-bit which he had in reserve. At length he produced it.

'Been seeing any more of your friend Norris?'

'Yes,' I said. 'Why?'

'Nothing,' drawled Fritz, his naughty eyes on my face. 'Eventually I'd watch your step, that's all.'

'Whatever do you mean?'

'I've been hearing some queer things about him.'

'Oh, indeed?'

'Maybe they aren't true. You know how people talk.'

'And I know how you listen, Fritz.'

He grinned; not in the least offended: 'There's a story going round that eventually Norris is some kind of cheap crook.'

'I must say, I should have thought that "cheap" was hardly a word one could apply to him.'

Fritz smiled a superior, indulgent smile.

'I dare say it would surprise you to know that he's been in prison?'

'What you mean is, it'd surprise me to know that your friends *say* he's been in prison. Well, it doesn't in the least. Your friends would say anything.'

Fritz didn't reply. He merely continued to smile.

'What's he supposed to have been in prison for?' I asked.

'I didn't hear,' Fritz drawled. 'But maybe I can guess.'

'Well, I can't.'

'Look, Bill, excuse me a moment.' He had changed his

40

tone now. He was serious. He laid his hand on my shoulder. 'What I mean to say, the thing is this. Eventually, we two, we don't give a damn, hell, for goodness' sake. But we've got other people to consider besides ourselves, haven't we? Suppose Norris gets hold of some kid and plucks him of his last cent?'

'How dreadful that would be.'

Fritz gave me up. His final shot was: 'Well, don't say I didn't warn you, that's all.'

'No, Fritz. I most certainly won't.'

We parted pleasantly.

Perhaps Helen Pratt had been right about me. Stage by stage I was building up a romantic background for Arthur, and was jealous lest it should be upset. Certainly, I rather enjoyed playing with the idea that he was, in fact, a dangerous criminal; but I am sure that I never seriously believed in it for a moment. Nearly every member of my generation is a crime-snob. I was fond of Arthur with an affection strengthened by obstinacy. If my friends didn't like him because of his mouth or his past, the loss was theirs; I was, I flattered myself, more profound, more humane, an altogether subtler connoisseur of human nature than they. And if, in my letters to England, I sometimes referred to him as 'a most amazing old crook,' I only meant by this that I wanted to imagine him as a glorified being; audacious and self-reliant, reckless and calm. All of which, in reality, he only too painfully and obviously wasn't.

Poor Arthur! I have seldom known anybody with such weak nerves. At times, I began to believe he must be suffering from a mild form of persecution mania. I can see him now as he used to sit waiting for me in the most secluded corner of our favourite restaurant, bored, abstracted, uneasy; his hands folded with studied nonchalance in his lap, his head held at an awkward, listening angle, as though he expected, at any moment, to be startled by a very loud bang. I can hear him at the telephone, speaking cautiously, as close as possible to the mouthpiece and barely raising his voice above a whisper.

'Hullo. Yes, it's me. So you've seen that party? Good. Now

when can we meet? Let's say at the usual time, at the house of the person who is interested. And please ask that other one to be there, too. No, no. Herr D. It's particularly important. Good-bye.'

I laughed. 'One would think, to hear you, that you were an arch-conspirator.'

'A *very* arch conspirator,' Arthur giggled. 'No, I assure you, my dear William, that I was discussing nothing more desperate than the sale of some old furniture in which I happen to be – er – financially interested.'

'Then why on earth all this secrecy?'

'One never knows who may be listening.'

'But, surely, in any case, it wouldn't interest them very much?'

'You can't be too careful nowadays,' said Arthur vaguely.

By this time, I had borrowed and read nearly all his 'amusing' books. Most of them were extremely disappointing. Their authors adopted a curiously prudish, snobby, lower-middle-class tone, and, despite their sincere efforts to be pornographic, became irritatingly vague in the most important passages. Arthur had a signed set of volumes of *My Life and Loves*. I asked him if he had known Frank Harris.

'Slightly, yes. It's some years ago now. The news of his death came as a great shock to me. He was a genius in his own way. So witty. I remember his saying to me, once, in the Louvre: "Ah, my dear Norris, you and I are the last of the gentleman adventurers." He could be very caustic, you know. People never forgot the things he said about them.

'And that reminds me,' continued Arthur meditatively, 'of a question once put to me by the late Lord Disley. "Mr Norris," he asked me, "are you an adventurer?"'

'What an extraordinary question. I don't call *that* witty. It was damned rude of him.'

'I replied: "We are all adventurers. Life is an adventure." Rather neat, don't you think?'

'Just the sort of answer he deserved.'

Arthur modestly regarded his finger-nails.

'I'm generally at my best in the witness-box.'

'Do you mean that this was during a trial?'

'Not a trial, William. An action. I was suing the *Evening Post* for libel.'

'Why, what had they said about you?'

'They had made certain insinuations about the conduct of a public fund with which I had been entrusted.'

'You won, of course?'

Arthur carefully stroked his chin. 'They were unable to make good their accusations. I was awarded five hundred pounds damages.'

'Have you often brought libel actions?'

'Five times,' Arthur modestly admitted. 'And on three other occasions the matter was settled out of court.'

'And you've always got damages?'

'Something. A mere bagatelle. Honour was satisfied.'

'It must be quite a source of income.'

Arthur made a deprecatory gesture. 'I should hardly go so far as to say that.'

This, at last, seemed the moment for my question.

'Tell me, Arthur. Have you ever been in prison?'

He rubbed his chin slowly, baring his ruined teeth. Into his vacant blue eyes came a curious expression. Relief, perhaps. Or even, I fancied, a certain gratified vanity.

'So you heard of the case?'

'Yes,' I lied.

'It was very widely reported at the time.' Arthur modestly arranged his hands upon the crook of his umbrella. 'Did you, by any chance, read a full account of the evidence?'

'No. Unfortunately not.'

'That's a pity. I should have had great pleasure in lending you the Press cuttings, but unfortunately they were lost in the course of one of my many moves. I should have liked to hear your impartial opinion ... I consider that the jury was unfairly prejudiced against me from the start. Had I had the experience which I have now I should have undoubtedly been acquitted. My counsel advised me quite wrongly. I should have pleaded justification, but he assured me that it would be quite impossible to obtain the necessary evidence. The judge was very hard on me. He even went so far as to insinuate that I had been engaged in a form of blackmail.'

'I say! That was going a bit far, wasn't it?'

'It was indeed.' Arthur shook his head sadly. 'The English legal mind is sometimes unfortunately unsubtle. It is unable to distinguish between the finer shades of conduct.'

'And how much ... how long did you get?'

'Eighteen months in the second division. At Wormwood Scrubs.'

'I hope they treated you properly?'

'They treated me in accordance with the regulations. I can't complain ... Nevertheless, since my release, I have felt a lively interest in penal reform. I make a point of subscribing to the various societies which exist for that purpose.'

There was a .pause, during which Arthur evidently indulged in painful memories. 'I think,' he continued at length, 'I may safely claim that in the course of my whole career I have very seldom, if ever, done anything which I knew to be contrary to the law ... On the other hand, I do and always shall maintain that it is the privilege of the richer but less mentally endowed members of the community to contribute to the upkeep of people like myself. I hope you're with me there?'

'Not being one of the richer members,' I said, 'yes.'

'I'm so glad. You know, William, I feel that we might come, in time, to see eye to eye upon many things ... It's quite extraordinary what a lot of good money is lying about, waiting to be picked up. Yes, positively picked up. Even nowadays. Only one must have the eyes to see it. And capital. A certain amount of capital is absolutely essential. One day I think I really must tell you about my dealings with an American who believed himself to be a direct descendant of Peter the Great. It's a most instructive story.'

Sometimes Arthur talked about his childhood. As a boy he was delicate and had never been sent to school. An only son, he lived alone with his widowed mother, whom he adored. Together they studied literature and art; together they visited Paris, Baden-Baden, Rome, moving always in the best society, from *Schloss* to *château*, from *château* to

44

palace, gentle, charming, appreciative; in a state of perpetual tender anxiety about each other's health. Lying ill in rooms with a connecting door, they would ask for their beds to be moved so that they could talk without raising their voices. Telling stories, making gay little jokes, they kept up each other's spirits through weary sleepless nights. Convalescent, they were propelled, side by side, in bath-chairs, through the gardens of Lucerne.

This invalid idyll was doomed, by its very nature, soon to end. Arthur had to grow up; to go to Oxford. His mother had to die. Sheltering him with her love to the very last, she refused to allow the servants to telegraph to him as long as she remained conscious. When at length they disobeyed her, it was too late. Her delicate son was spared, as she had intended, the strain of a death-bed farewell.

After her death, his health improved greatly, for he had to stand on his own feet. This novel and painful attitude was considerably eased by the small fortune he had inherited. He had money enough to last him, according to the standards of social London in the 'nineties, for at least ten years. He spent it in rather less than two. 'It was at that time,' said Arthur, 'that I first learnt the meaning of the word "luxury." Since then, I am sorry to say, I have been forced to add others to my vocabulary; horrid ugly ones, some of them.' 'I wish,' he remarked simply, on another occasion, 'I had that money now. I should know what to do with it.' In those days he was only twenty-two and didn't know. It disappeared with magic speed into the mouths of horses and the stockings of ballet girls. The palms of servants closed on it with an oily iron grip. It was transformed into wonderful suits of clothes which he presented after a week or two, in disgust, to his valet; into oriental knick-knacks which somehow, when he got them back to his flat, turned out to be rusty old iron pots; into landscapes of the latest impressionist genius which by daylight next morning were childish daubs. Well groomed and witty, with money to burn, he must have been one of the most eligible young bachelors of his large circle; but it was the money lenders, not the ladies, who got him in the end.

A stern uncle, appealed to, grudgingly rescued him, but imposed conditions. Arthur was to settle down to read for the Bar. 'And I can honestly say that I did try. I can't tell you the agonies I suffered. After a month or two I was compelled to take steps.' When I asked what the steps were, he became uncommunicative. I gathered that he had found some way of putting his social connections to good use. 'It seemed very sordid at the time,' he added cryptically. 'I was such a very sensitive young man, you know. It makes one smile to think of it now.

'From that moment I date the beginning of my career; and, unlike Lot's wife, I have never looked back. There have been ups and downs ... ups and downs. The ups are a matter of European history. The downs I prefer not to remember. Well, well. As the proverbial Irishman said, I have put my hand to the plough and now I must lie on it.'

During that spring and early summer, Arthur's ups and downs were, I gathered, pretty frequent. He was never very willing to discuss them; but his spirits always sufficiently indicated the state of his finances. The sale of the 'old furniture' (or whatever it really was) seemed to provide a temporary respite. And, in May, he returned from a short trip to Paris very cheerful, having, as he guardedly said, 'several little irons in the fire.'

Behind all these transactions moved the sinister, pumpkin-headed figure of Schmidt. Arthur was quite frankly afraid of his secretary, and no wonder. Schmidt was altogether too useful; he had made his master's interests identical with his own. He was one of those people who have not only a capacity, but a positive appetite for doing their employer's dirty work. From chance remarks made by Arthur in less discreet moments, I was gradually able to form a fair idea of the secretary's duties and talents. 'It is very painful for any-one of our own class to say certain things to certain in-dividuals. It offends our delicate sensibilities. One has to be so very crude.' Schmidt, it seemed, experienced no pain. He was quite prepared to say anything to anybody. He con-fronted creditors with the courage and technique of a bullfighter. He followed up the results of Arthur's wildest shots, and returned with money like a retriever bringing home a duck.

Schmidt controlled and doled out Arthur's pocket-money. Arthur wouldn't, for a long time, admit this; but it was obvious. There were days when he hadn't enough to pay his bus fare; others when he would say: 'Just a moment, William. I shall have to run up to my flat to fetch something I'd forgotten. You won't mind waiting down here a minute, will you?' On such occasions, he would rejoin me, after a quarter of an hour or so, in the street; sometimes deeply depressed, sometimes radiant, like a schoolboy who has received an unexpectedly large tip.

Another phrase to which I became accustomed was: 'I'm afraid I can't ask you to come up just now. The flat's so untidy.' I soon discovered this to mean that Schmidt was at home. Arthur, who dreaded scenes, was always at pains to prevent our meeting; for, since my first visit, our mutual dislike had considerably increased. Schmidt, I think, not only disliked me, but definitely disapproved of me as a hostile and unsettling influence on his employer. He was never exactly offensive. He merely smiled his insulting smile and amused himself by coming suddenly into the room on his noiseless shoes. He would stand there a few seconds, unnoticed, and then speak, startling Arthur into a jump and a little scream. When he had done this two or three times in succession, Arthur's nerves would be in such a state that he could no longer talk coherently about anything and we had to retire to the nearest café to continue our conversation. Schmidt would help his master on with his overcoat and bow us out of the flat with ironic ceremony, slyly content that his object had been achieved.

In June, we went to spend a long week-end with Baron von Pregnitz; he had invited us to his country villa, which stood on the shore of a lake in Mecklenburg. The largest room in the villa was a gymnasium fitted with the most modern apparatus, for the Baron made a hobby of his figure. He tortured himself daily on an electric horse, a rowing-

47

machine and a rotating massage belt. It was very hot and we all bathed, even Arthur. He wore a rubber swimming-cap, carefully adjusted in the privacy of his bedroom. The house was full of handsome young men with superbly developed brown bodies which they smeared in oil and baked for hours in the sun. They ate like wolves and had table manners which pained Arthur deeply; most of them spoke with the broadest Berlin accents. They wrestled and boxed on the beach and did somersault dives from the springboard into the lake. The Baron joined in everything and often got severely handled. With good-humoured brutality the boys played practical jokes on him which smashed his spare monocles and might easily have broken his neck. He bore it all with his heroic frozen smile.

On the second evening of our visit, he escaped from them and took a walk with me in the woods, alone. That morning they had tossed him in a blanket and he had landed on the asphalt pavement; he was still a bit shaky. His hand rested heavily on my arm. 'When you get to my age,' he told me sadly, 'I think you will find that the most beautiful things in life belong to the Spirit. The Flesh alone cannot give us happiness.' He sighed and gave my arm a faint squeeze.

'Our friend Kuno is a most remarkable man,' observed Arthur, as we sat together in the train on our way back to Berlin. 'Some people believe that he has a great career ahead of him. I shouldn't be at all surprised if he were to be offered an important post under the next Government.'

'You don't say so?'

'I think,' Arthur gave me a discreet, sideways glance, 'that he's taken a great fancy to you.'

'Do you?'

'I sometimes feel, William, that with your talents, it's a pity you're not more ambitious. A young man should make use of his opportunities. Kuno is in a position to help you in all sorts of ways.'

I laughed. 'To help both of us, you mean?'

'Well, if you put it in that way, yes. I quite admit that I foresee certain advantages to myself from the arrangement.

Whatever my faults, I hope I'm not a hypocrite. For instance, he might make you his secretary.'

'I'm sorry, Arthur,' I said, 'but I'm afraid I should find my duties too heavy.'

Towards the end of August, Arthur left Berlin. An air of mystery surrounded his departure; he hadn't even told me that he was thinking of going. I rang up the flat twice, at times when I was pretty sure Schmidt would not be there. Hermann, the cook, knew only that his master was away for an indefinite period. On the second occasion, I asked where he had gone, and was told London. I began to be afraid that Arthur had left Germany for good. No doubt he had the best of reasons for doing so.

One day, however, during the second week in September, the telephone rang. Arthur himself was on the line.

'Is that you, dear boy? Here I am, back at last! I've got such a lot to tell you. Please don't say you're engaged this evening. You aren't? Then will you come round here about half-past six? I think I may add that I've got a little surprise in store for you. No, I shan't tell you anything more. You must come and see for yourself. *Au revoir.*'

I arrived at the flat to find Arthur in the best of spirits.

'My dear William, what a pleasure to see you again! How have you been getting on? Getting on and getting off?'

Arthur tittered, scratched his chin and glanced rapidly and uneasily round the room as though he were not yet quite convinced that all the furniture was still in its proper place.

'What was it like in London?' I asked. In spite of what he had said over the telephone, he didn't seem in a particularly communicative mood.

'In London?' Arthur looked blank. 'Ah, yes. London ... To be perfectly frank with you, William, I was not in London. I was in Paris. Just at present, it is desirable that a slight uncertainty as to my whereabouts should exist in the minds of certain persons here.' He paused, added impressively: 'I suppose I may tell you, as a very dear and intimate

50

friend, that my visit was not unconnected with the Communist Party.'

'Do you mean to say that you've become a communist?'

'In all but name, William, yes. In all but name.'

He paused for a moment, enjoying my astonishment. 'What is more, I asked you here this evening to witness what I may call my Confessio Fidei. In an hour's time, I am due to speak at a meeting held to protest against the exploitation of the Chinese peasantry. I hope you'll do me the honour of coming.'

'Need you ask?'

The meeting was to be held in Neukölln. Arthur insisted on taking a taxi all the way. He was in an extravagant mood.

'I feel,' he remarked, 'that I shall look back on this evening as one of the turning-points of my career.'

He was visibly nervous and kept fingering his bunch of papers. Occasionally he cast an unhappy glance out of the taxi window, as though he would have liked to ask the driver to stop.

'I should think your career has had a good many turning-points,' I said, to distract his thoughts.

Arthur brightened at once at the implied flattery.

'It has, William. It has, indeed. If my life were going to end tonight (which I sincerely hope it won't) I could truthfully say: At any rate, I have lived ... I wish you had known me in the old days, in Paris, just before the War. I had my own car and an apartment on the Bois. It was one of the show places of its kind. The bedroom I designed myself, all in crimson and black. My collection of whips was probably unique.' Arthur sighed. 'Mine is a sensitive nature. I react immediately to my surroundings. When the sun shines on me, I expand. To see me at my best, you must see me in my proper setting. A good table. A good cellar. Art. Music. Beautiful things. Charming and witty society. Then I begin to sparkle. I am transformed.'

The taxi stopped. Arthur fussily paid the driver, and we passed through a large beer-garden, now dark and empty, into a deserted restaurant, where an elderly waiter informed us that the meeting was being held upstairs. 'Not the first door,' he added. 'That's the Skittles Club.'

'Oh dear,' exclaimed Arthur, 'I'm afraid we must be very late.'

He was right. The meeting had already begun. As we climbed the broad rickety staircase, we could hear the voice of a speaker echoing down the long shabby corridor. Two powerfully built youths wearing hammer-and-sickle armlets kept guard at the double doors. Arthur whispered a hurried explanation, and they let us pass. He pressed my hand nervously. 'I'll see you later, then.' I sat down on the nearest available chair.

The hall was large and cold. Decorated in tawdry baroque, it might have been built about thirty years ago and not re-painted since. On the ceiling, an immense pink, blue and gold design of cherubim, roses and clouds was peeled and patched with damp. Round the walls were draped scarlet banners with white lettering: '*Arbeiterfront gegen Fascismus und Krieg.*' '*Wir fordern Arbeit und Brot.*' '*Arbeiter aller Länder, vereinigt euch.*'

The speaker sat at a long table on the stage facing the audience. Behind them, a tattered backcloth represented a forest glade. There were two Chinese, a girl who was taking shorthand notes, a gaunt man with fuzzy hair who propped his head in his hands, as if listening to music. In front of them, dangerously near the edge of the platform, stood a short, broad-shouldered, red-haired man, waving a piece of paper at us like a flag.

'Those are the figures, comrades. You've heard them. They speak for themselves, don't they? I needn't say any more. Tomorrow you'll see them in print in the *Welt am Abend*. It's no good looking for them in the capitalist Press, because they won't be there. The bosses will keep them out of their newspapers, because, if they were published, they might upset the stock exchanges. Wouldn't that be a pity? Never mind. The workers will read them. The workers will know what to think of them. Let's send a message to our comrades in China: The workers of the German Communist Party protest against the outrages of the Japanese murderers.

The workers demand assistance for the hundreds of thousands of Chinese peasants now rendered homeless. Comrades, the Chinese section of the I.A.H. appeals to us for funds to fight Japanese imperialism and European exploitation. It's our duty to help them. We're going to help them.'

The red-haired man smiled as he spoke, a militant, triumphant smile; his white, even teeth gleamed in the lamplight. His gestures were slight but astonishingly forceful. At moments it seemed as if the giant energy stored up in his short, stocky frame would have flung him bodily from the platform, like an over-powerful motor-bicycle. I had seen his photograph two or three times in the newspaper, but couldn't remember who he was. From where I sat, it was difficult to hear everything he said. His voice drowned itself, filling the large, damp hall with thundering echoes.

Arthur now appeared upon the stage, shaking hands hastily with the Chinese, apologizing, fussing to his chair. A burst of applause which followed the red-haired man's last sentence visibly startled him. He sat down abruptly.

During the clapping, I moved up several rows in order to hear better, squeezing into a place I had seen was empty in front of me. As I sat down, I felt a tug at my sleeve. It was Anni, the girl with the boots. Beside her, I recognized the boy who had poured the beer down Kuno's throat at Olga's on New Year's Eve. They both seemed pleased to see me. The boy shook hands with a grip which nearly made me yell out loud.

The hall was very full. The audience sat there in their soiled everyday clothes. Most of the men wore breeches with coarse woollen stockings, sweaters and peaked caps. Their eyes followed the speaker with hungry curiosity. I had never been to a communist meeting before, and what struck me most was the fixed attention of the upturned rows of faces; faces of the Berlin working class, pale and prematurely lined, often haggard and ascetic, like the heads of scholars, with thin, fair hair brushed back from their broad foreheads. They had not come here to see each other or to be seen, or even to fulfil a social duty. They were attentive but not passive. They were not spectators. They participated, with a curious, restrained passion, in the speech made by the red-haired man. He spoke for them, he made their thoughts articulate. They were listening to their own collective voice. At intervals they applauded it, with sudden, spontaneous violence. Their passion, their strength of purpose elated me. I stood outside it. One day, perhaps, I should be with it, but never of it. At present I just sat there, a half-hearted renegade from my own class, my feelings muddled by anarchism talked at Cambridge, by slogans from the confirmation service, by the tunes the band played when my father's regiment marched to the railway station, seventeen years ago. And the little man finished his speech and went back to his place at the table amidst thunders of clapping.

'Who is he?' I asked.

'Why, don't you know?' exclaimed Anni's friend in surprise. 'That's Ludwig Bayer. One of the best men we've got.'

The boy's name was Otto. Anni introduced us and I got another crushing hand-squeeze. Otto changed places with her so that he could talk to me.

'Were you at the Sport Palace the other night? Man, you ought to have heard him! He spoke for two hours and a half without so much as a drink of water.'

A Chinese delegate now stood up and was introduced. He spoke careful, academic German. In sentences which were like the faint, plaintive twanging of an Asiatic musical instrument, he told us of the famine, of the great floods, of the Japanese air-raids on helpless towns. 'German comrades, I bring you a sad message from my unhappy country.'

'My word!' whispered Otto, impressed. 'It must be worse there than at my aunt's in the Simeonstrasse.'

It was already a quarter past nine. The Chinese was followed by the man with fuzzy hair. Arthur was becoming impatient. He kept glancing at his watch and furtively touching his wig. Then came the second Chinese. His German was inferior to that of his colleague, but the audience followed the speeches as eagerly as ever. Arthur, I could see, was nearly frantic. At length, he got up and went round to the back of Bayer's chair. Bending over, he began speaking in an agitated whisper. Bayer smiled and made a friendly, soothing gesture.

He seemed amused. Arthur returned dubiously to his place, where he soon began to fidget again.

The Chinese finished at last. Bayer at once stood up, took Arthur encouragingly by the arm, as though he were a mere boy, and led him to the front of the stage.

'This is the comrade Arthur Norris, who has come to speak to us about the crimes of British Imperialism in the Far East.'

It seemed so absurd to me to see him standing there that I could hardly keep a straight face. Indeed, it was difficult for me to understand why everybody in the hall didn't burst out laughing. But no, the audience evidently didn't find Arthur in the least funny. Even Anni, who had more reason than anyone present to regard him from a comic angle, was perfectly grave.

Arthur coughed, shuffled his papers. Then he began to speak in his fluent, elaborate German, a little too fast:

'Since that day on which the leaders of the allied governments saw fit, in their infinite wisdom, to draw up that, no doubt, divinely inspired document known as the Treaty of Versailles; since that day, I repeat ...'

A slight stir, as if of uneasiness, passed over the rows of listeners. But the pale, serious, upturned faces were not ironic. They accepted without question this urbane bourgeois gentleman, accepted his stylish clothes, his graceful *rentier* wit. He had come to help them. Bayer had spoken for him. He was their friend.

'British Imperialism has been engaged, during the last two hundred years, in conferring upon its victims the dubious benefits of the Bible, the Bottle and the Bomb. And of these three, I might perhaps venture to add, the Bomb has been infinitely the least noxious.'

There was applause at this; delayed, hesitant clapping, as if Arthur's hearers approved his matter, but were still doubtful of his manner. Evidently encouraged, he continued:

'I am reminded of the story of the Englishman, the German and the Frenchman who had a wager as to which of them could cut down the most trees in one day. The Frenchman was the first to try ...'

At the end of this story there was laughter and loud applause. Otto thumped me violently on the back in his delight. *'Mensch! Der spricht prima, wahr?'* Then he bent forward again to listen, his eyes intent upon the platform, his arm round Anni's shoulder. Arthur exchanging his graceful bantering tone for an oratorical seriousness, was approaching his climax:

'The cries of the starving Chinese peasantry are ringing in our ears as we sit in this hall tonight. They have come to us across the breadth of the world. Soon, we hope, they will sound yet more loudly, drowning the futile chatter of diplomatists and the strains of dance bands in luxurious hotels, where the wives of armament manufacturers finger the pearls which have been bought with the price of the blood of innocent children. Yes, we must see to it that those cries are clearly heard by every thinking man and woman in Europe and America. For then, and only then, will a term be set to this inhuman exploitation, this traffic in living souls . . .'

Arthur concluded his speech with an energetic flourish. His face was quite flushed. Salvo upon salvo of clapping rattled over the hall. Many of the audience cheered. While the applause was still at its height, Arthur came down from the platform and joined me at the doors. Heads were turned to watch us go out. Otto and Anni had left the meeting with us. Otto wrung Arthur's hand and dealt him terrific blows on the shoulder with his heavy palm: 'Arthur, you old house! That was fine!'

'Thank you, my dear boy. Thank you.' Arthur winced. He was feeling very pleased with himself. 'How did they take it, William? Well, I think? I hope I made my points quite clearly? Please say I did.'

'Honestly, Arthur, I was astounded.'

'How charming of you; praise from such a severe critic as yourself is indeed music to my ears.'

'I'd no idea you were such an old hand at it.'

'In my time,' admitted Arthur modestly, 'I've had occasion to do a good deal of public speaking, though hardly quite of this kind.'

We had cold supper at the flat. Schmidt and Hermann

were both out; Otto and Anni made tea and laid the table. They seemed quite at home in the kitchen and knew where everything was kept.

'Otto is Anni's chosen protector,' Arthur explained, while they were out of the room. 'In another walk of life, one would call him her impresario. I believe he takes a certain percentage of her earnings. I prefer not to inquire too closely. He's a nice boy, but excessively jealous. Luckily, not of Anni's customers. I should be very sorry indeed to get into his bad books. I understand that he's the middle-weight champion of his boxing club.'

At length the meal was ready. He fussed round, giving directions.

'Will the Comradess Anni bring us some glasses? How nice of her. I should like to celebrate this evening. Perhaps, if Comrade Otto would be so kind, we might even have a little brandy. I don't know whether Comrade Bradshaw drinks brandy. You'd better ask him.'

'At such an historic moment, Comrade Norris, I drink anything.'

Otto came back to report that there was no more brandy.

'Never mind,' said Arthur, 'brandy is not a proletarian drink. We'll drink beer.' He filled our glasses. 'To the world revolution.'

'To the world revolution.'

Our glasses touched. Anni sipped daintily, holding the glass-stem between finger and thumb, her little finger mincingly crooked. Otto drained his at a gulp, banging down the tumbler heartily on to the table. Arthur's beer went the wrong way and choked him. He coughed, spluttered, dived for his napkin.

'I'm afraid that's an evil omen,' I said jokingly. He seemed quite upset.

'Please don't say that, William. I don't like people to say things of that kind, even in jest.'

This was the first time I had ever known Arthur to be superstitious. I was amused and rather impressed. He appeared to have got it badly. Could he really have undergone a sort of religious conversion? It was difficult to believe.

'Have you been a communist long, Arthur?' I asked, in English, as we began to eat.

He cleared his throat slightly, shot an uneasy glance in the direction of the door.

'At heart, William, yes. I think I may say that I have always felt that, in the deepest sense, we are all brothers. Class distinctions have never meant anything to me; and hatred of tyranny is in my blood. Even as a small child, I could never bear injustice of any kind. It offends my sense of the beautiful. It is so stupid and unæsthetic. I remember my feelings when I was first unjustly punished by my nurse. It wasn't the punishment itself which I resented; it was the clumsiness, the lack of imagination behind it. That, I remember, pained me very deeply.'

'Then why didn't you join the Party long ago?'

Arthur looked suddenly vague; stroked his temples with his finger-tips:

'The time was not ripe. No.'

'And what does Schmidt say to all this?' I asked mischievously.

Arthur gave the door a second hurried glance. As I had suspected, he was in a state of suspense lest his secretary should suddenly walk in upon us.

'I'm afraid Schmidt and I don't quite see eye to eye on the subject just at present.'

I grinned. 'No doubt you'll convert him in time.'

'Shut up talking English, you two,' cried Otto, giving me a vigorous jog in the ribs. 'Anni and I want to hear the joke.'

During supper we drank a good deal of beer. I must have been rather unsteady on my feet, because when I stood up at the end of the meal, I knocked over my chair. On the under-side of the seat was pasted a ticket with the printed number 69.

'What's this for?' I asked.

'Oh that?' said Arthur hastily; he seemed very much disconcerted. 'That's merely the catalogue number from the sale where I originally bought it. It must have been there all this time ... Anni, my love, do you think you and Otto would be so very kind as to carry some of the things into the kitchen

58

and put them in the sink? I don't like to leave Hermann too much to do in the morning. It makes him cross with me for the rest of the day.'

'What is that ticket for?' I repeated gently, as soon as they were outside. 'I want to know.'

Arthur sadly shook his head.

'Ah, my dear William, nothing escapes your eye. Yet another of our domestic secrets is laid bare.'

'I'm afraid I'm very dense. What secret?'

'I rejoice to see that your young life has never been sullied by such sordid experiences. At your age, I regret to say, I had already made the acquaintance of the gentleman whose sign-manual you will find upon every piece of furniture in this room.'

'Good God, do you mean the bailiff?'

'I prefer the word *Gerichtsvollzieher*. It sounds so much nicer.'

'But, Arthur, when is he coming?'

'He comes, I'm sorry to say, almost every morning. Sometimes in the afternoon as well. He seldom finds me at home, however. I prefer to let Schmidt receive him. From what I have seen of him, he seems a person of little or no culture. I doubt if we should have anything in common.'

'Won't he soon be taking everything away?'

Arthur seemed to enjoy my dismay. He puffed at his cigarette with exaggerated nonchalance.

'On Monday next, I believe.'

'How frightful! Can't anything be done about it?'

'Oh, undoubtedly something can be done about it. Something *will* be done about it. I shall be compelled to pay another visit to my Scotch friend, Mr Isaacs. Mr Isaacs assures me that he comes of an old Scotch family, the Inverness Isaacs. The first time I had the pleasure of meeting him, he nearly embraced me: "Ah, my dear Mr Norris," he said, "you are a countryman of mine." '

'But, Arthur, if you go to a moneylender, you'll only get into worse trouble still. Has this been going on for long? I always imagined that you were quite rich.'

Arthur laughed:

'I am rich, I hope, in the things of the Spirit ... My dear boy, please don't alarm yourself on my account. I've been living on my wits for nearly thirty years now, and I propose to continue doing so until such time as I am called into the, I'm afraid, not altogether approving company of my fathers.'

Before I could ask any more questions, Anni and Otto returned from the kitchen. Arthur greeted them gaily and soon Anni was sitting on his knee, resisting his advances with slaps and bites, while Otto, having taken off his coat and rolled up his sleeves, was absorbed in trying to repair the gramophone. There seemed no place for myself in this domestic tableau and I soon said that I must be going.

Otto came downstairs with a key to let me out of the house door. In parting, he gravely raised his clenched fist in salute:

'Red Front.'

'Red Front,' I answered.

CHAPTER SIX

One morning, not long after this, Frl. Schroeder came shuffling into my room in great haste, to tell me that Arthur was on the telephone.

'It must be something very serious. Herr Norris didn't even say good morning to me.' She was impressed and rather hurt.

'Hullo, Arthur. What's the matter?'

'For Heaven's sake, my dear boy, don't ask me any questions now.' His tone was nervously irritable and he spoke so rapidly that I could barely understand him. 'It's more than I can bear. All I want to know is, can you come here at once?'

'Well ... I've got a pupil coming at ten o'clock.'

'Can't you put him off?'

'Is it as important as all that?'

Arthur uttered a little cry of peevish exasperation: 'Is it important? My dear William, do please endeavour to exercise your imagination. Should I be ringing you up at this unearthly hour if it wasn't important? All I beg of you is a plain answer: Yes or No. If it's a question of money, I shall be only too glad to pay you your usual fee. How much do you charge?'

'Shut up, Arthur, and don't be absurd. If it's urgent, of course I'll come. I'll be with you in twenty minutes.'

I found all the doors of the flat standing open, and walked in unannounced: Arthur, it appeared, had been rushing wildly from room to room like a flustered hen. At the moment, he was in the sitting-room dressed ready to go out, and nervously pulling on his gloves. Hermann, on his knees, rummaged sulkily in a cupboard in the hall. Schmidt lounged in the doorway of the study, a cigarette between his lips. He did not make the least effort to help and was evidently enjoying his employer's distress.

'Ah, here you are, William, at last!' cried Arthur, on seeing me. 'I thought you were never coming. Oh dear, oh dear! Is it as late as that already? Never mind about my grey hat. Come along, William, come along. I'll explain everything to you on the way.'

Schmidt gave us an unpleasant, sarcastic smile as we went out.

When we were comfortably settled on the top of a bus, Arthur became calmer and more coherent.

'First of all,' he fumbled rapidly in all his pockets and produced a folded piece of paper: 'Please read that.'

I looked at it. It was a *Vorladung* from the Political Police. Herr Arthur Norris was requested to present himself at the Alexanderplatz that morning before one o'clock. What would happen should he fail to do so was not stated. The wording was official and coldly polite.

'Good God, Arthur,' I said, 'whatever does this mean? What have you been up to now?'

In spite of his nervous alarm, Arthur displayed a certain modest pride.

'I flatter myself that my association with,' he lowered his voice and glanced quickly at our fellow passengers, 'the representatives of the Third International has not been entirely unfruitful. I am told that my efforts have even excited favourable comment in certain quarters in Moscow ... I told you, didn't I, that I'd been in Paris? Yes, yes, of course ... Well, I had a little mission there to fulfil. I spoke to certain highly placed individuals and brought back certain instructions ... Never mind that now. At all events, it appears that the authorities here are better informed than we'd supposed. That is what I have to find out. The whole question is extremely delicate. I must be careful not to give anything away.'

'Perhaps they'll put you through the third degree.'

'Oh, William, how can you say anything so dreadful? You make me feel quite faint.'

'But, Arthur, surely that would be ... I mean, wouldn't you rather enjoy it?'

Arthur giggled: 'Ha, ha. Ha, ha. I must say this, William, that even in the darkest hour your humour never fails to restore me ... Well, well, perhaps if the examination were to be conducted by Frl. Anni, or some equally charming young lady, I might undergo it with – er – very mixed feelings. Yes.' Uneasily he scratched his chin. 'I shall need your moral support. You must come and hold my hand. And if this,' he glanced nervously over his shoulder, 'interview should terminate unpleasantly, I shall ask you to go to Bayer and tell him exactly what has happened.'

'Yes, I will. Of course.'

When we had got out of the bus on the Alexanderplatz, poor Arthur was so shaky that I suggested going into a restaurant and drinking a glass of cognac. Seated at a little table we regarded the immense drab mass of the Praesidium buildings from the opposite side of the roadway.

'The enemy fortress,' said Arthur, 'into which poor little I have got to venture, all alone.'

'Remember David and Goliath.'

'Oh, dear. I'm afraid the Psalmist and I have very little in common this morning. I feel more like a beetle about to be squashed by a steam-roller ... It's a curious fact that, since my earliest years, I have had an instinctive dislike of the police. The very cut of their uniforms offends me, and the German helmets are not only hideous but somehow rather sinister. Merely to see one of them filling in an official form in that inhuman copy-book handwriting gives me a sinking feeling in the stomach.'

'Yes, I know what you mean.'

Arthur brightened a little.

'I'm very glad I've got you with me, William. You have such a sympathetic manner. I could wish for no better companion on the morning of my execution. The very opposite of that odious Schmidt, who simply gloats over my misfortune. Nothing makes him happier than to be in a position to say – I told you so.'

'After all, there's nothing very much they can do to you in there. They only knock workmen about. Remember, you belong to the same class as their masters. You must make them feel that.'

'I'll try,' said Arthur doubtfully.

'Have another cognac?'

'Perhaps I will, yes.'

The second cognac worked wonders. We emerged from the restaurant into the still, clammy autumn morning, laughing, arm in arm.

'Be brave, Comrade Norris. Think of Lenin.'

'I'm afraid, ha, ha, I find more inspiration in the Marquis de Sade.'

But the atmosphere of the police headquarters sobered him considerably. Increasingly apprehensive and depressed, we wandered along vistas of stone passages with numbered doors, were misdirected up and down flights of stairs, collided with hurrying officials who carried bulging dossiers of crimes. At length we came out into a courtyard, overlooked by windows with heavy iron bars.

'Oh dear, oh dear!' moaned Arthur. 'We've put our heads into the trap this time, I'm afraid.'

At this moment a piercing whistle sounded from above.

'Hullo, Arthur!'

Looking down from one of the barred windows high above was Otto.

'What did they get you for?' he shouted, jocularly. Before either of us could answer, a figure in uniform appeared beside him at the window and hustled him away. The apparition was as brief as it was disconcerting.

'They seem to have rounded up the whole gang,' I said, grinning.

'It's certainly very extraordinary,' said Arthur, much perturbed. 'I wonder if ...'

We passed under an archway, up more stairs, into a honeycomb of little rooms and dark passages. On each floor were wash-basins, painted a sanitary green. Arthur consulted his *Vorladung* and found the number of the room in which he was to present himself. We parted in hurried whispers.

'Good-bye, Arthur. Good luck. I'll wait for you here.'

'Thank you, dear boy ... And supposing the worst comes to the worst, and I emerge from this room in custody, don't speak to me or make any sign that you know me unless I speak to you. It may be advisable not to involve you ...

here's Bayer's address; in case you have to go there alone.'

'I'm certain I shan't.'

'There's one more thing I wanted to say to you.' Arthur had the manner of one who mounts the steps of the scaffold. 'I'm sorry if I was a little hasty over the telephone this morning. I was very much upset . . . If this were to be our last meeting for some time, I shouldn't like you to remember it against me.'

'What rubbish, Arthur. Of course I shan't. Now run along, and let's get this over.'

He pressed my hand, knocked timidly at the door and went in.

I sat down to wait for him, under a blood-red poster advertising the reward for betraying a murderer. My bench was shared by a fat Jewish slum-lawyer and his client, a tearful little prostitute.

'All you've got to remember,' he kept telling her, 'is that you never saw him again after the night of the sixth.'

'But they'll get it out of me somehow,' she sobbed, 'I know they will. It's the way they look at you. And then they ask you a question so suddenly. You've no time to think.'

It was nearly an hour before Arthur reappeared. I could see at once from his face that the interview hadn't been so bad as he'd anticipated. He was in a great hurry.

'Come along, William. Come along. I don't care to stay here any longer than I need.'

Outside in the street, he hailed a taxi and told the chauffeur to drive to the Hotel Kaiserhof, adding, as he nearly always did:

'There's no need to drive too fast.'

'The Kaiserhof!' I exclaimed. 'Are we going to pay a call on Hitler?'

'No, William. We are not . . . although, I admit, I derive a certain pleasure from dallying in the camp of the enemy. Do you know, I have lately made a point of being manicured there? They have a very good man. Today, however, I have a quite different object. Bayer's office is also in the Wilhelmstrasse. It didn't seem altogether discreet to drive directly from here to there.'

Accordingly, we performed the comedy of entering the hotel, drinking a cup of coffee in the lounge and glancing through the morning papers. To my disappointment, we didn't see Hitler or any of the other Nazi leaders. Ten minutes later, we came out again into the street. I found myself squinting rapidly to right and left, in search of possible detectives. Arthur's police-obsession was exceedingly catching.

Bayer inhabited a large untidy flat on the top floor of one of the shabbier houses beyond the Zimmerstrasse. It was certainly a striking enough contrast to what Arthur called 'the camp of the enemy,' the padded, sombre, luxurious hotel we had just left. The door of the flat stood permanently ajar. Inside, the walls were hung with posters in German and Russian, notices of mass meetings and demonstrations, anti-war cartoons, maps of industrial areas and graphs to illustrate the dimensions and progress of strikes. There were no carpets on the bare unpainted floor-boards. The rooms echoed to the rattle of typewriters. Men and women of all ages wandered in and out or sat chatting on upturned sugar-boxes waiting for interviews; patient, good-humoured, quite at home. Everybody seemed to know everybody; a newcomer was greeted almost invariably by his or her Christian name. Even strangers were addressed as Thou. Cigarette smoking was general. The floors were littered with crushed-out stubs.

In the midst of this informal, cheerful activity, we found Bayer himself, in a tiny shabby room, dictating a letter to the girl whom I had seen on the platform at the meeting in Neukölln. He seemed pleased but not especially surprised to see Arthur.

'Ah, my dear Norris. And what can I do for you?'

He spoke English with great emphasis and a strong foreign accent. I thought I had never seen anybody with such beautiful teeth. Indeed, his teeth and Arthur's were both, in their different ways, so remarkable that the two sets might have been placed side by side, as classic contrasts, in a dental museum.

'You have been already to see them?' he added.

'Yes,' said Arthur. 'We've just come from there.'

The girl secretary got up and went out, closing the door

behind her. Arthur, his elegantly gloved hands resting demurely in his lap, began to describe his interview with the
officials at the Polizeipraesidium. Bayer sat back in his chair
and listened. He had extraordinarily vivid animal eyes of a
dark reddish brown. His glance was direct, challenging, brilliant as if with laughter, but his lips did not even smile.
Listening to Arthur, his face and body became quite still. He
did not once nod, or shift his position, or fidget with his
hands. His mere repose suggested a force of concentration
which was hypnotic in its intensity. Arthur, I could see,
felt this also; he squirmed uneasily on his seat and carefully avoided looking Bayer in the eyes.

Arthur began by assuring us that the officials had treated
him most politely. One of them had helped him off with
his coat and hat, the other had offered him a chair and a
cigar. Arthur had taken the chair, the cigar he had refused;
he made a considerable point of this, as though it were
a proof of his singular strong-mindedness and integrity.
Thereupon, the official, still courteous, had asked permission
to smoke. This Arthur had granted.

There had followed a discussion, cross-examination dis-
guised as chat, about Arthur's business activities in Berlin.
Arthur was careful not to go into details here. 'It wouldn't
interest you,' he told Bayer. I gathered, however, that the
officials had politely succeeded in frightening him a good
deal. They were far too well informed.

These preliminaries over, the real questioning began. 'We
understand, Mr Norris, that you have recently made a journey
to Paris. Was this visit in connection with your private
business?'

Arthur had been ready for this, of course. Perhaps too
ready. His explanations had been copious. The official had
punctured them with a single affable inquiry. He had named
a name and an address which Mr Norris had twice visited,
on the evening of his arrival and on the morning of his departure. Was this, also, a private business interview? Arthur
didn't deny that he had had a nasty shock. Nevertheless, he
had been, he claimed, exceedingly discreet. 'I wasn't so silly as
to deny anything, of course. I made light of the whole matter.

I think I impressed them favourably. They were shaken, I could see that, distinctly shaken.'

Arthur paused, added modestly: 'I flatter myself that I know how to handle that particular kind of situation pretty well. Yes.'

His tone appealed for a word of encouragement, of confirmation, here. But Bayer didn't encourage, didn't condemn, didn't speak or move at all. His dark brown eyes continued to regard Arthur with the same brilliant attention, smiling and alert. Arthur uttered a short nervous cough.

Anxious to interest that impersonal, hypnotic silence, he made a great deal of his narrative. He must have talked for nearly half an hour. Actually, there wasn't much to tell. The police, having displayed the extent of their knowledge, had hastened to assure Mr Norris that his activities did not interest them in the least, provided that these activities were confined to foreign countries. As for Germany itself, that, of course, was a different matter. The German Republic welcomes all foreign guests, but requires them to remember that certain laws of hospitality govern guest as well as host. In short, it would be a great pity if the German Republic were ever to be deprived of the pleasure of Mr Norris' society. The official felt sure that Mr Norris, as a man of the world, would appreciate his point of view.

Finally, just as Arthur was making for the door, having been helped on with his overcoat and presented with his hat, came a last question asked in a tone which suggested that it hadn't the remotest connection with anything which had previously been said:

'You have recently become a member of the Communist Party?'

'I saw the trap at once, of course,' Arthur told us. 'It was simply a trap. But I had to think quickly; any hesitation in answering would have been fatal. They're so accustomed to notice these details ... I am not a member of the Communist Party, I said to them, nor of any other Left Wing organization. I merely sympathize with the attitude of the K.P.D. to certain non-political problems ... I think that was the right answer? I think so. Yes.'

At last Bayer both smiled and spoke. 'You have acted quite right, my dear Norris.' He seemed subtly amused.

Arthur was as pleased as a stroked cat.

'Comrade Bradshaw was of great assistance to me.'

'Oh yes?'

Bayer didn't ask how.

'You have interest for our movement?'

His eyes measured me for the first time. No, he was not impressed. Equally, he did not condemn. A young bourgeois intellectual, he thought. Enthusiastic, within certain limits. Educated, within certain limits. Capable of response if appealed to in terms of his own class-language. Of some small use: everybody can do something. I felt myself blushing deeply.

'I'd like to help you if I could,' I said.

'You speak German?'

'He speaks excellent German,' put in Arthur, like a mother recommending her son to the notice of the headmaster. Smilingly, Bayer considered me once more.

'So?'

He turned over the papers on his desk.

'Here is some translation which you could be so kind as to do for us. Will you please translate this in English? As you will see, it is a report of our work during the past year. From it you will learn a little about our aims. It should interest you, I think.'

He handed me a thick wad of manuscript, and rose to his feet. He was even smaller and broader than he had seemed on the platform. He laid a hand on Arthur's shoulder.

'This is most interesting, what you have told me.' He shook hands with both of us, gave a brilliant parting smile: 'And you will please,' he added comically to Arthur, 'avoid to entangle this young Mr Bradshaw in your distress.'

'Indeed, I assure you I shouldn't dream of such a thing. His safety is almost, if not quite, as dear to me as my own ... Well, ha ha, I won't waste any more of your valuable time. Good-bye.'

The interview with Bayer had quite restored Arthur's spirits.

'You made a good impression on him, William. Oh yes, you did. I could see that at once. And he's a very shrewd judge of character. I think he was pleased with what I said to them at the Alexanderplatz, wasn't he?'

'I'm sure he was.'

'I think so, yes.'

'Who is he?' I asked.

'I know very little about him, myself, William. I've heard that he began life as a research chemist. I don't think his parents were working people. He doesn't give one that impression, does he? In any case, Bayer isn't his real name.'

After this meeting, I felt anxious to see Bayer again. I did the translation as quickly as I could, in the intervals of giving lessons. It took me two days. The manuscript was a report on the aims and progress of various strikes, and the measures taken to supply food and clothing to the families of the strikers. My chief difficulty was with the numerous and ever-recurring groups of initial letters which represented the names of the different organizations involved. As I did not know what most of these organizations were called in English, I didn't know what letters to substitute for those in the manuscript.

'It is not so important,' replied Bayer, when I asked him about this. 'We will attend to this matter ourselves.'

Something in his tone made me feel humiliated. The manuscript he had given me to translate was simply not important. It would probably never be sent to England at all. Bayer had given it me, like a toy, to play with, hoping, no doubt, to be rid of my tiresome, useless enthusiasm for a week at least.

'You find this work interesting?' he continued. 'I am glad. It is necessary for every man and woman in our days to have knowledge of this problem. You have read something from Marx?'

I said that I had once tried to read *Das Kapital*.

'Ah, that is too difficult, for a beginning. You should try the *Communist Manifesto*. And some of Lenin's pamphlets. Wait, I will give you ...'

He was amiability itself. He seemed in no hurry to get

70

rid of me. Could it really be that he had no more important way of spending the afternoon? He asked about the living conditions in the East End of London and I tried to eke out the little knowledge I had collected in the course of a few days' slumming, three years before. His mere attention was flattery of the most stimulating kind. I found myself doing nearly all the talking. Half an hour later, with books and more papers to translate under my arm, I was about to say good-bye when Bayer asked:

'You have known Norris a long time?'

'More than a year, now,' I replied, automatically, my mind registering no reaction to the question.

'Indeed? And where did you meet?'

This time I did not miss the tone in his voice. I looked hard at him. But his extraordinary eyes were neither suspicious, nor threatening, nor sly. Smiling pleasantly, he simply waited in silence for my answer.

'We got to know each other in the train, on the way to Berlin.'

Bayer's glance became faintly amused. With disarming, bland directness, he asked:

'You are good friends? You go to see him often?'

'Oh yes. Very often.'

'You have not many English friends in Berlin, I think?'

'No.'

Bayer nodded seriously. Then he rose from his chair and shook my hand. 'I have to go now and work. If there is anything you wish to say to me, please do not hesitate to come and see me at any time.'

'Thank you very much.'

So that was it, I thought, on my way down the shabby staircase. None of them trusted Arthur. Bayer didn't trust him, but he was prepared to make use of him, with all due precautions. And to make use of me, too, as a convenient spy on Arthur's movements. It wasn't necessary to let me into the secret. I could so easily be pumped. I felt angry, and at the same time rather amused.

After all, one couldn't blame them.

CHAPTER SEVEN

Otto turned up at Arthur's about a week later, unshaven and badly in need of a meal. They had let him out of prison the day before. When I went round to the flat that evening, I found him with Arthur in the dining-room, having just finished a substantial supper.

'And what did they used to give you on Sundays?' he was asking as I came in. 'We got pea-soup with a sausage in it. Not so bad.'

'Let me see now,' Arthur reflected. 'I'm afraid I really can't remember. In any case, I never had much appetite ... Ah, my dear William, here you are! Please take a chair. That is, if you don't disdain the company of two old gaol-birds. Otto and I were just comparing notes.'

The day before Arthur and I visited the Alexanderplatz, Otto and Anni had had a quarrel. Otto had wanted to give fifteen pfennigs to a man who came round collecting for a strike fund of the I.A.H. Anni had refused to agree to this, 'on principle.' 'Why should the dirty communists have my money?' she had said. 'I have to work hard enough to earn it.' The possessive pronoun challenged Otto's accepted status and rights; he generously disregarded it. But the adjective had really shocked him. He had slapped her face, 'not hard,' he assured us, but violently enough to make her turn a somersault over the bed and land with her head against the wall; the bump had dislodged a framed photograph of Stalin, which had fallen to the ground and smashed its glass. Anni had begun to curse him and cry. 'That'll teach you not to talk about things you don't understand,' Otto had told her, not unkindly. Communism had always been a delicate subject between them. 'I'm sick of you,' cried Anni, 'and all your bloody Reds. Get out of here!' She had thrown the photograph-frame at him and missed.

Thinking all this over carefully, in the neighbouring *Lokal*,

Otto had come to the conclusion that he was the injured party. Pained and angry, he began drinking *Korn*. He drank a good deal. He was still drinking at nine o'clock in the evening, when a boy named Erich, whom he knew, came in, selling biscuits. Erich, with his basket, went the rounds of the cafés and restaurants in the whole district, carrying messages and picking up gossip. He told Otto that he had just seen Anni in a Nazi *Lokal* on the Kreuzberg, with Werner Baldow.

Werner was an old enemy of Otto's, both political and private. A year ago, he had left the communist cell to which Otto belonged and joined the local Nazi storm-troop. He had always been sweet on Anni. Otto, who was pretty drunk by this time, did what even he would never have dared when sober; he jumped up and set off for the Nazi *Lokal* alone. Two policemen who happened to pass the place a minute or two after he entered it probably saved him from getting broken bones. He had just been flung out for the second time and wanted to go in again. The policemen removed him with difficulty; he bit and kicked on the way to the station. The Nazis, of course, were virtuously indignant. The incident featured in their newspapers next day as 'an unprovoked and cowardly attack on a National-Socialist *Lokal* by ten armed communists, nine of whom made a successful escape.' Otto had the cutting in his pocket-book and showed it to us with pride. He had been unable to get at Werner himself. Werner had retreated with Anni into a room at the back of the *Lokal* as soon as he had come in.

'And he can keep her, the dirty bitch,' added Otto violently. 'I wouldn't have her again if she came to me on her knees.'

'Well, well,' Arthur began to murmur automatically, 'we live in stirring times ...'

He pulled himself up abruptly. Something was wrong. His eyes wandered uneasily over the array of plates and dishes, like an actor deprived of his cue. There was no tea-pot on the table.

Not many days after this, Arthur telephoned to tell me that Otto and Anni had made it up.

'I felt sure you'd be glad to hear. I may say that I myself

was to some extent instrumental in the good work. Yes ... Blessed are the peacemakers ... As a matter of fact, I was particularly interested in effecting a reconciliation just now, in view of a little anniversary which falls due next Wednesday ... You didn't know? Yes, I shall be fifty-three. Thank you, dear boy. Thank you. I must confess I find it difficult to become accustomed to the thought that the yellow leaf is upon me ... And now, may I invite you to a trifling banquet? The fair sex will be represented. Besides the reunited pair, there will be Madame Olga and two other of my more doubtful and charming acquaintances. I shall have the sitting-room carpet taken up, so that the younger members of the party can dance. Is that nice?'

'Very nice indeed.'

On Wednesday evening I had to give an unexpected lesson and arrived at Arthur's flat later than I intended. I found Hermann waiting downstairs at the house door to let me in.

'I'm so sorry,' I said. 'I hope you haven't been standing here long?'

'It's all right,' Hermann answered briefly. He unlocked the door and led the way upstairs. What a dreary creature he is, I thought. He can't even brighten up for a birthday party.

I discovered Arthur in the sitting-room. He was reclining on the sofa in his shirt-sleeves, his hands folded in his lap.

'Here you are, William.'

'Arthur, I'm most terribly sorry. I hurried as much as I could. I thought I should never get away. That old girl I told you about arrived unexpectedly and insisted on having a two-hour lesson. She merely wanted to tell me about the way her daughter had been behaving. I thought she'd never stop ... Why, what's the matter? You don't look well.'

Arthur sadly scratched his chin.

'I'm very depressed, dear boy.'

'But why? What about? ... I say, where are your other guests? Haven't they come yet?'

'They came. I was obliged to send them away.'

'Then you *are* ill?'

'No, William. Not ill. I fear I'm getting old. I have always

74

hated scenes and now I find them altogether too much for me.'

'Who's been making a scene?'

Arthur raised himself slowly from his chair. I had a sudden glimpse of him as he would be in twenty years' time; shaky and rather pathetic.

'It's a long story, William. Shall we have something to eat first? I'm afraid I can only offer you scrambled eggs and beer; if indeed there is any beer.'

'It doesn't matter if there isn't. I've brought you a little present.'

I produced a bottle of cognac which I had been holding behind my back.

'My dear boy, you overwhelm me. You shouldn't, you know. You really shouldn't. Are you sure you can afford it?'

'Oh yes, easily. I'm saving quite a lot of money nowadays.'

'I always,' Arthur shook his head sadly, 'look upon the capacity to save money as little short of miraculous.'

Our footsteps echoed loudly where the carpet had been.

'All was prepared for the festivities, when the spectre appeared to forbid the feast,' Arthur chuckled nervously and rubbed his hands together.

'Ah, but the Apparition, the dumb sign,
The beckoning finger bidding me forgo,
The fellowship, the converse and the wine,
The songs, the festal glow!

'Rather apt here, I think. I hope you know your William Watson? I have always regarded him as the greatest of the moderns.'

The dining-room was draped with paper festoons in preparation for the party; Chinese lanterns were suspended above the table. On seeing them, Arthur shook his head.

'Shall we have these things taken down, William? Will they depress you too much, do you think?'

'I don't see why they should,' I said. 'On the contrary, they ought to cheer us up. After all, whatever has happened, it's still your birthday.'

'Well, well. You may be right. You're always so philosophical. The blows of fate are indeed cruel.'

Hermann gloomily brought in the eggs. He reported, with rather bitter satisfaction, that there was no butter.

'No butter,' Arthur repeated. 'No butter. My humiliation as a host is complete ... Who would think, to see me now, that I have entertained more than one member of a royal family under my own roof? This evening, I had intended to set a sumptuous repast before you. I won't make your mouth water by reciting the menu.'

'I think the eggs are very nice. I'm only sorry that you had to send your guests away.'

'So am I, William. So am I. Unfortunately, it was impossible to ask them to stay. I shouldn't have dared face Anni's displeasure. She was naturally expecting to find a groaning board ... And, in any case, Hermann told me there weren't enough eggs in the house.'

'Arthur, do tell me now what has happened?'

He smiled at my impatience, enjoying a mystery, as always. Thoughtfully, he squeezed his collapsed chin between finger and thumb.

'Well, William, the somewhat sordid story which I am about to relate to you centres on the sitting-room carpet.'

'Which you had taken up for the dancing?'

Arthur shook his head.

'It was not, I regret to say, taken up for the dancing. That was merely a *façon de parler*. I didn't wish to distress one of your sympathetic nature unnecessarily.'

'You mean, you've sold it?'

'Not sold, William. You should know me better. I never sell if I can pawn.'

'I'm sorry. It was a nice carpet.'

'It was, indeed ... And worth very much more than the two hundred marks I got for it. But one mustn't expect too much these days ... At all events, it would have covered the expenses of the little celebration I had planned. Unfortunately,' here Arthur glanced towards the door, 'the eagle, or, shall I say, the vulture eye of Schmidt lighted upon the vacant space left by the carpet, and his uncanny acumen rejected almost immediately the very plausible explanation which I gave for its disappearance. He was very cruel to me. Very firm ... To cut a long story short, I was left, at the end of our most unpleasant interview, with the sum of four marks, seventy-five pfennigs. The last twenty-five pfennigs were an unfortunate after-thought. He wanted them for his bus-fare home.'

'He actually took away your money?'

'Yes, it *was* my money, wasn't it?' said Arthur, eagerly, seizing this little crumb of encouragement. 'That's just what I told him. But he only shouted at me in the most dreadful way.'

'I never heard anything like it. I wonder you don't sack him.'

'Well, William, I'll tell you. The reason is very simple. I owe him nine months' wages.'

'Yes, I supposed there was something like that. All the same, it's no reason why you should allow yourself to be shouted at. I wouldn't have put up with it.'

'Ah, my dear boy, you're always so firm. I only wish I'd had you there to protect me. I feel sure you would have been able to deal with him. Although I must say,' Arthur added doubtfully, 'Schmidt can be terribly firm when he likes.'

'But, Arthur, do you seriously mean to tell me that you intended spending two hundred marks on a dinner for seven people? I never heard anything so fantastic.'

'There were to have been little presents,' said Arthur meekly. 'Something for each of you.'

'It would have been lovely, of course ... But such extravagance ... You're so hard up that you can only eat eggs, and yet, when you do get some cash, you propose to blow it immediately.'

'Don't *you* start lecturing me, too, William, or I shall cry. I can't help my little weaknesses. Life would be drab indeed if we didn't sometimes allow ourselves a treat.'

'All right,' I said, laughing. 'I won't lecture you. In your place, I'd probably have done just the same.'

After supper, when we had returned with the cognac into the denuded sitting-room, I asked Arthur if he had seen

Bayer lately. The change which came over his face at the mention of the name surprised me. His soft mouth pursed peevishly. Avoiding my glance, he frowned and abruptly shook his head.

'I don't go there more than I can help.'

'Why?'

I had seldom seen him like this. He seemed, indeed, annoyed with me for having asked the question. For a moment he was silent. Then he broke out, with childish petulance:

'I don't go there because I don't like to go. Because it upsets me to go. The disorder in that office is terrible. It depresses me. It offends a person of my sensibilities to see such entire lack of method ... Do you know, the other day Bayer lost a most important document, and where do you think it was found? In the waste-paper basket. Actually ... to think that these people's wages are paid out of the hard-earned savings of the workers. It makes one's blood boil ... And, of course, the whole place is infested with spies. Bayer even knows their names ... And what does he do about it? Nothing. Absolutely nothing. He doesn't seem to care. That's what so infuriates me; that happy-go-lucky way of doing things. Why, in Russia, they'd simply be put against the wall and shot.'

I grinned. Arthur as the militant revolutionary was a little too good to be true.

'You used to admire him so much.'

'Oh, he's an able enough man in his way. No doubt about that.' Arthur furtively rubbed his chin. His teeth were bared in the snarl of an old lion. 'I've been very much disappointed in Bayer,' he added.

'Indeed?'

'Yes.' Some last vestiges of caution visibly held him back. But no. The temptation was too exquisite: 'William, if I tell you something, you must promise on all you hold sacred that it will go no farther.'

'I promise.'

'Very well. When I threw in my lot with the Party, or, rather, promised it my help (and though I say it who shouldn't, I am in a position to help them in many quarters to which they have not hitherto had access)—'

'I'm sure you are.

'I stipulated, very naturally I think, for a (how shall I put it?) – let us say – a *quid pro quo*.' Arthur paused and glanced at me anxiously. 'I hope, William, that that doesn't shock you?'

'Not in the least.'

'I'm very glad. I might have known that you'd look at the thing in a sensible light ... After all, one's a man of the world. Flags and banners and catchwords are all very well for the rank and file, but the leaders know that a political campaign can't be carried on without money. I talked this over with Bayer at the time when I was considering taking the plunge, and, I must say, he was very reasonable about it. He quite saw that, crippled as I am with five thousand pounds' worth of debts ...'

'My God, is it as much as that?'

'It is, I'm sorry to say. Of course, not all my engagements are equally pressing ... Where was I? Yes. Crippled as I am with debts I am hardly in a position to be of much service to the Cause. As you know yourself, I am subject to all sorts of vulgar embarrassments.'

'And Bayer agreed to pay some of them?'

'You put things with your usual directness, William. Well, yes, I may say that he hinted, most distinctly hinted, that Moscow would not be ungrateful if I fulfilled my first mission successfully. I did so. Bayer would be the first to admit that. And what has happened? Nothing. Of course, I know it's not altogether his fault. His own salary and that of the typists and clerks in his office is often months overdue. But it's none the less annoying for that. And I can't help feeling that he doesn't press my claim as much as he might. He even seems to regard it as rather funny when I come to him and complain that I've barely enough money for my next meal ... Do you know, I'm still owed for my trip to Paris? I had to pay the fare out of my own pocket; and imagining, naturally enough, that the expenses, at least, would be defrayed, I travelled first class.'

'Poor Arthur!' I had some trouble to avoid laughing. 'And

what shall you do now? Is there any prospect of this money coming after all?'

'I should think none,' said Arthur gloomily.

'Look here, let me lend you some. I've got ten marks.'

'No, thank you, William. I appreciate the thought, but I couldn't borrow from you. I feel that it would spoil our beautiful friendship. No, I shall wait two days more; then I shall take certain steps. And, if these are not successful, I shall know what to do.'

'You're very mysterious.' For an instant, the thought even passed through my mind that Arthur was perhaps meditating suicide. But the very idea of his attempting to kill himself was so absurd that it made me begin to smile. 'I hope everything will go off all right,' I added, as we said good-bye.

'So do I, my dear William. So do I.' Arthur glanced cautiously down the staircase. 'Please give my regards to the divine Schroeder.'

'You really must come and visit us some day soon. It's such a long time since you've been. She's pining away without you.'

'With the greatest pleasure, when all these troubles are over. If they ever are.' Arthur sighed deeply. 'Good night, dear boy. God bless you.'

CHAPTER EIGHT

The next day, Thursday, I was busy with lessons. On Friday, I tried three times to ring up Arthur's flat, but the number was always engaged. On Saturday, I went away for the week-end to see some friends in Hamburg. I didn't get back to Berlin until late on Monday afternoon. That evening I dialled Arthur's number, wanting to tell him about my visit; again there was no reply. I rang four times, at intervals of half an hour, and then complained to the operator. She told me, in official language, that 'the subscriber's instrument' was 'no longer in use.'

I wasn't particularly surprised. In the present state of Arthur's finances, it was hardly to be expected that he would have settled his telephone bill. All the same, I thought, he might have come to see me or sent a note. But no doubt he was busy, too.

Three more days went by. It was seldom that we had ever let a whole week pass without a meeting or, at any rate, a telephone conversation. Perhaps Arthur was ill. Indeed, the more I thought about it, the surer I felt that this must be the explanation of his silence. He had probably worried himself into a nervous breakdown over his debts. And, all this while, I had been neglecting him. I felt suddenly very guilty. I would go round and see him, I decided that same afternoon.

Some premonition or pang of conscience made me hurry. I reached the Courbierestrasse in record time, ran quickly up-stairs, and, still panting, rang the bell. After all, Arthur was no longer young. The life he had been leading was enough to break anybody down; and he had a weak heart. I must be prepared to hear serious news. Supposing ... hullo, what was this? In my haste, I must have miscounted the number of floors. I was standing in front of a door without a name-plate; the door of a strange flat. It was one of those silly embarrassing things which always happen when one lets oneself get flustered. My first impulse was to run away, up or down stairs, I wasn't quite sure which. But, after all, I had rung these people's bell. The best thing would be to wait until somebody answered it, and then explain my mistake.

I waited; one minute, two, three. The door didn't open. There was nobody at home, it seemed. I had been saved from making a fool of myself, after all.

But now I noticed something else. On both the doors which faced me were little squares of paint which were darker than the rest of the woodwork. There was no doubt about it; they were the marks left by recently removed name-plates. I could even see the tiny holes where the screws had been. A kind of panic seized me. Within half a minute, I had run up the stairs to the top of the house, then down again to the bottom; very quickly and lightly, as one sometimes runs in a nightmare. Arthur's two name-plates were nowhere to be found. But wait: perhaps I was in the wrong house altogether. I had done stupider things before now. I went out into the street and looked at the number over the entrance. No, there was no mistake there.

I don't know what I mightn't have done, at that moment, if the portress herself hadn't appeared. She knew me by sight and nodded ungraciously. She plainly hadn't much use for Arthur's callers. No doubt the visits of the bailiff had got the house a bad name.

'If you're looking for your friend,' she maliciously emphasized the word, 'you're too late. He's gone.'

'Gone?'

'Yes. Two days ago. The flat's to let. Didn't you know?'

I suppose my face was a comic picture of dismay, for she added unpleasantly: 'You aren't the only one he didn't tell. There've been a dozen round here already. Owed you some money, did he?'

'Where's he gone to?' I asked dully.

'I'm sure I don't know, or care. That cook of his comes round here and collects the letters. You'd better ask him.'

'I can't. I don't know where he lives.'

'Then I can't help you,' said the portress with a certain

vicious satisfaction. Arthur must have neglected to tip her. 'Why don't you try the police?'

With this parting shot she went into her lodge and slammed the door. I walked slowly away down the street, feeling rather dazed.

My question was soon answered, however. The next morning I got a letter, dated from an hotel in Prague:

My dear William,

Do forgive me. I was compelled to leave Berlin at very short notice and under conditions of secrecy which made it impossible for me to communicate with you. The little *operation* about which I spoke to you was, alas, the reverse of successful, and the doctor ordered an immediate *change of air*. So *unhealthy*, indeed, had the atmosphere of Berlin become for one of my peculiar constitution, that, had I remained another week, *dangerous complications* would almost certainly have arisen.

My *lares* and *penates* have all been sold and the proceeds largely swallowed up by the demands of my various satellites. I don't complain of that. They have, with *one* exception, served me faithfully, and the labourer is worthy of his hire. As for that *one*, I shall not permit his odious name to pass my lips again. Suffice it to say that he was and is a scoundrel of the *deepest dye* and has behaved as such.

I find life here very pleasant. The cooking is good, not so good as in my beloved and incomparable Paris, whither I hope, next Wednesday, to wend my weary steps, but still far better than anything which barbarous Berlin could provide. Nor are the consolations of the fair and *cruel* sex absent. Already, under the grateful influence of civilized comfort, I put forth my leaves, I expand. To such an extent, indeed, have I already expanded that I fear I shall arrive in Paris almost devoid of means. Never mind. The Mammon of Unrighteousness will, no doubt, be ready to receive me into habitations which, if not everlasting, will at least give me time to look round.

Please convey to our mutual friend my most fraternal greetings and tell him that I shall not fail, on arriving, to execute his various commissions.

Do write soon and regale me with your inimitable wit.

As always, your affectionate

ARTHUR.

My first reaction was to feel, perhaps unreasonably, angry. I had to admit to myself that my feeling for Arthur had been largely possessive. He was my discovery, my property. I was as hurt as a spinster who has been deserted by her cat. And yet, after all, how silly of me. Arthur was his own master; he wasn't accountable to me for his actions. I began to look round for excuses for his conduct, and, like an indulgent parent, easily found them. Hadn't he, indeed, behaved with considerable nobility? Threatened from every side, he had faced his troubles alone. He had carefully avoided involving me in possible future unpleasantness with the authorities. After all, he had said to himself, I am leaving this country, but William has to stay here and earn his living; I have no right to indulge my personal feelings at his expense. I pictured Arthur taking a last hurried stroll down our street, glancing up with furtive sadness at the window of my room, hesitating, walking sorrowfully away. The end of it was that I sat down and wrote him a chatty, affectionate letter, asking no questions and, indeed, avoiding any remark which might compromise either him or myself. Frl. Schroeder, who was much upset at the news of Arthur's departure, added a long postscript. He was never to forget, she wrote, that there was *one* house in Berlin where he would always be welcome.

My curiosity was far from being satisfied. The obvious thing was to question Otto, but where was I to find him? I decided to try Olga's for a start. Anni, I knew, rented a bedroom there.

I hadn't seen Olga since that party in the small hours of the New Year; but Arthur, who sometimes visited her in the way of business, had told me a good deal about her from time to time. Like most people who still contrived to earn a living in those bankrupt days, she was a woman of numerous occupations. 'Not to put too fine a point upon it,' as Arthur was fond of saying, she was a procuress, a cocaine-seller and a receiver of stolen goods; she also let lodgings, took in washing and, when in the mood, did exquisite fancy needlework. Arthur once showed me a table-centre she had given him for Christmas which was quite a work of art.

I found the house without difficulty and passed under the archway into the court. The courtyard was narrow and deep, like a coffin standing on end. The head of the coffin rested on the earth, for the house-fronts inclined slightly inwards. They were held apart by huge timber baulks, spanning the gap, high up, against the grey square of sky. Down here, at the bottom, where the rays of the sun could never penetrate, there was a deep twilight, like the light in a mountain gorge. On three sides of the court were windows; on the fourth, an immense blank wall, about eighty feet high, whose plaster surface had swollen into blisters and burst, leaving raw, sooty scars. At the foot of this ghastly precipice stood a queer little hut, probably an outdoor lavatory. Beside it was a broken hand-cart with only one wheel, and a printed notice, now almost illegible, stating the hours at which the inhabitants of the tenement were allowed to beat their carpets.

The staircase, even at this hour of the afternoon, was very dark. I stumbled up it, counting the landings, and knocked at a door which I hoped was the right one. There was a shuffle of slippers, a clink of keys, and the door opened a little way, on the chain.

'Who's there?' a woman's voice asked.

'William,' I said.

The name made no impression. The door began, doubtfully, to shut.

'A friend of Arthur's,' I added hastily, trying to make my voice sound reassuring. I couldn't see what sort of person I was talking to; inside the flat it was pitch black. It was like speaking to a priest in a confessional.

'Wait a minute,' said the voice.

The door shut and the slippers shuffled away. Other footsteps returned. The door reopened and the electric light was switched on in the narrow hall. On the threshold stood

Olga herself. Her mighty form was enveloped in a kimono of garish colours which she wore with the majesty of a priestess in her ceremonial robes. I hadn't remembered her as being quite so enormous.

'Well?' she said. 'What do you want?'

She hadn't recognized me. For all she knew I might be a detective. Her tone was aggressive and harsh; it showed not the least trace of hesitation or fear. She was ready for all her enemies. Her hard blue eyes, ceaselessly watchful as the eyes of a tigress, moved away over my shoulder into the gloomy well of the staircase. She was wondering whether I had come alone.

'May I speak to Frl. Anni?' I said politely.

'You can't. She's busy.'

My English accent had reassured her, however; for she added briefly: 'Come inside,' and turned, leading the way into the sitting-room. She left me with entire indifference to shut the outer door. I did so meekly and followed.

Standing on the sitting-room table was Otto, in his shirt-sleeves, tinkering with the converted gasolier.

'Why, it's Willi!' he cried, jumping down and dealing me a staggering clap on the shoulder.

We shook hands. Olga lowered herself into a chair facing mine with the deliberation and sinister dignity of a fortune-teller. The bracelets jangled harshly on her swollen wrists. I wondered how old she was; perhaps not more than thirty-five, for there were no wrinkles on her puffy, waxen face. I didn't much like her hearing what I had to say to Otto, but she had plainly no intention of moving as long as I was in the flat. Her blue doll's eyes held mine in a brutal, unwinking regard.

'Haven't I seen you somewhere before?'

'You've seen me in this room,' I said, 'drunk.'

'So.' Olga's bosom shook silently. She had laughed.

'Did you see Arthur before he left?' I asked Otto, at the end of a long pause.

Yes, Anni and Otto had both seen him, though quite by chance, as it appeared. Happening to look in on the Sunday afternoon, they had discovered Arthur in the midst of his packing. There had been a great deal of telephoning and running hither and thither. And then Schmidt had appeared. He and Arthur had retired into the bedroom for a conference, and soon Otto and Anni had heard loud, angry voices. Schmidt had come out of the bedroom, with Arthur following him in a state of ineffectual rage. Otto hadn't been able to understand very clearly what it was all about, but the Baron had had something to do with it, and money. Arthur was angry because of something Schmidt had said to the Baron; Schmidt was insulting and contemptuous by turns. Arthur had cried: 'You've shown not only the blackest ingratitude, but downright treachery!' Otto was quite positive about this. The phrase seemed to have made a special impression on him; perhaps because the word 'treachery' had a definitely political flavour in his mind. Indeed, he quite took it for granted that Schmidt had somehow betrayed the Communist Party. 'The very first time I saw him, I said to Anni, "I shouldn't wonder if he's been sent to spy on Arthur. He looks like a Nazi, with that great big swollen head of his."'

What followed had confirmed Otto in his opinion. Schmidt had been just about to leave the flat when he turned and said to Arthur:

'Well, I'm off. I'll leave you to the tender mercies of your precious communist friends. And when they've swindled you out of your last pfennig ...'

He hadn't got any farther. For Otto, puzzled by all this talk and relieved at last to hear something which he could understand and resent, had taken Schmidt out of the flat by the back of the collar and sent him flying downstairs with a hearty kick on the bottom. Otto, in his narrative, dwelt on the kick with special pride and pleasure. It had been one of the kicks of his life, an inspired kick, beautifully judged and timed. He was anxious that I should understand just how and where it had landed. He made me stand up, and touched me lightly on the buttock with his toe. I was a little uneasy, knowing what an effort of self-control it cost him not to let fly.

'My word, Willi, you should have heard him land! Bing! Bong! Crash! For a minute he didn't seem to know where he was or what had happened to him. And then he began to blubber, just like a baby. I was so weak with laughing at him you could have pushed me downstairs with one finger.'

And Otto began to laugh now, as he said it. He laughed heartily, without the least malice or savagery. He bore the discomfited Schmidt no grudge.

I asked whether anything more had been heard of him. Otto didn't know. Schmidt had picked himself up, slowly and painfully, sobbed out some inarticulate threat, and limped away downstairs. And Arthur, who had been present in the background, had shaken his head doubtfully and protested.

'You shouldn't have done that, you know.'

'Arthur's much too kind-hearted,' added Otto, coming to the end of his story. 'He trusts everybody. And what thanks does he get for it? None. He's always being swindled and betrayed.'

No comment on this last remark seemed adequate. I said that I must be going.

Something about me seemed to amuse Olga. Her bosom silently quivered. Without warning, as we reached the door, she gave my cheek a rough, deliberate pinch, as though she were plucking a plum from a tree.

'You're a nice boy,' she chuckled harshly. 'You must come round here one evening. I'll teach you something you didn't know before.'

'You ought to try it once with Olga, Willi,' Otto seriously advised. 'It's well worth the money.'

'I'm sure it is,' I said politely, and hurried downstairs.

A few day later, I had a rendezvous with Fritz Wendel at the Troika. Arriving rather too early, I sat down at the bar and found the Baron on the stool next to my own.

'Hullo, Kuno!'

'Good evening.'

He inclined his sleek head stiffly. To my surprise, he didn't seem at all pleased to see me. Indeed, quite the reverse. His monocle gleamed polite hostility; his naked eye was evasive and shifty.

'I haven't seen you for ages,' I said brightly, trying to appear serenely unconscious of his manner.

His eye travelled round the room; he was positively searching for help, but nobody answered his appeal. The place was still nearly empty. The barman edged over towards us.

'What'll you have to drink?' I asked. His dislike of my society was beginning to intrigue me.

'Er – nothing, thank you. You see, I have to be going.'

'What, you're leaving us so soon, Herr Baron?' put in the barman affably; unconsciously adding to his discomfort: 'Why, you've hardly been here five minutes, you know.'

'Have you heard from Arthur Norris?' With deliberate malice I disregarded his attempts to dismount from his stool. He couldn't do so until I had pushed mine back a little.

The name made Kuno visibly wince.

'No.' His tone was icy. 'I have not.'

'He's in Paris, you know.'

'Indeed?'

'Well,' I said heartily. 'I mustn't keep you any longer.'

I held out my hand. He barely touched it.

'Good-bye.'

Released at last, he made like an arrow for the door. One might have thought that he was escaping from a plague hospital. The barman, discreetly smiling, picked up the coins and shovelled them into the till. He had seen spongers snubbed before.

I was left with another mystery to solve.

Like a long train which stops at every dingy little station, the winter dragged slowly past. Each week there were new emergency decrees. Brüning's weary episcopal voice issued commands to the shopkeepers, and was not obeyed. 'It's Fascism,' complained the Social Democrats. 'He's weak,' said Helen Pratt. 'What these swine need is a man with hair on his chest.' The Hessen Document was discovered; but nobody really cared. There had been one scandal too many. The exhausted public had been fed with surprises to point of indigestion. People said that the Nazis would be in power by Christmas; but Christmas came and they were not. Arthur sent me the compliments of the season on a postcard of the Eiffel Tower.

Berlin was in a state of civil war. Hate exploded suddenly, without warning, out of nowhere; at street corners, in restaurants, cinemas, dance halls, swimming-baths; at midnight, after breakfast, in the middle of the afternoon. Knives were whipped out, blows were dealt with spiked rings, beer-mugs, chair-legs or leaded clubs; bullets slashed the advertisements on the poster-columns, rebounded from the iron roofs of latrines. In the middle of a crowded street a young man would be attacked, stripped, thrashed and left bleeding on the pavement; in fifteen seconds it was all over and the assailants had disappeared. Otto got a gash over the eye with a razor in a battle on a fair-ground near the Cöpernickerstrasse. The doctor put in three stitches and he was in hospital for a week. The newspapers were full of death-bed photographs of rival martyrs, Nazi, Reichsbanner and Communist. My pupils looked at them and shook their heads, apologizing to me for the state of Germany. 'Dear, dear!' they said, 'it's terrible. It can't go on.'

The murder reporters and the jazz-writers had inflated the German language beyond recall. The vocabulary of newspaper invective (traitor, Versailles-lackey, murder-swine, Marx-crook, Hitler-swamp, Red-pest) had come to resemble, through excessive use, the formal phraseology of politeness employed by the Chinese. The word *Liebe*, soaring from the Goethe standard, was no longer worth a whore's kiss. *Spring, moonlight, youth, roses, girl, darling, heart, May:* such was the miserably devaluated currency dealt in by the authors of all those tangoes, waltzes and fox-trots which advocated the private escape. Find a dear little sweetheart, they advised, and forget the slump, ignore the unemployed. Fly, they urged us, to Hawaii, to Naples, to the Never-Never-Vienna. Hugenberg, behind the Ufa, was serving up nationalism to suit all tastes. He produced battlefield epics, farces of barrack-room life, operettas in which the jinks of a pre-war military aristocracy were reclothed in the fashions of 1932. His brilliant directors and cameramen had to concentrate their talents on cynically beautiful shots of the bubbles in champagne and the sheen of lamplight on silk.

And morning after morning, all over the immense, damp,

dreary town and the packing-case colonies of huts in the suburb allotments, young men were waking up to another workless empty day to be spent as they could best contrive; selling bootlaces, begging, playing draughts in the hall of the Labour Exchange, hanging about urinals, opening the doors of cars, helping with crates in the markets, gossiping, lounging, stealing, overhearing racing tips, sharing stumps of cigarette-ends picked up in the gutter, singing folk-songs for groschen in courtyards and between stations in the carriages of the Underground Railway. After the New Year, the snow fell, but did not lie; there was no money to be earned by sweeping it away. The shopkeepers rang all coins on the counter for fear of the forgers. Frl. Schroeder's astrologer foretold the end of the world. 'Listen,' said Fritz Wendel, between sips of a cocktail in the bar of the Eden Hotel, 'I give a damn if this country goes communist. What I mean, we'd have to alter our ideas a bit. Hell, who cares?'

At the beginning of March, the posters for the Presidential Election began to appear. Hindenburg's portrait, with an inscription in gothic lettering beneath it, struck a frankly religious note: 'He hath kept faith with you; be ye faithful unto Him.' The Nazis managed to evolve a formula which dealt cleverly with this venerable icon and avoided the offence of blasphemy: 'Honour Hindenburg; Vote for Hitler.' Otto and his comrades set out every night, with paint-pots and brushes, on dangerous expeditions. They climbed high walls, scrambled along roofs, squirmed under hoardings; avoiding the police and the S.A. patrols. And next morning, passersby would see Thälmann's name boldly inscribed in some prominent and inaccessible position. Otto gave me a bunch of little gum-backed labels: Vote for Thälmann, the Workers' Candidate. I carried these about in my pocket and stuck them on shop-windows and doors when nobody was looking.

Brüning spoke in the Sport Palace. We must vote for Hindenburg, he told us, and save Germany. His gestures were sharp and admonitory; his spectacles gleamed emotion in the limelight. His voice quivered with dry academic passion. 'Inflation,' he threatened, and the audience shuddered.

'Tannenberg,' he reverently reminded: there was prolonged applause.

Bayer spoke in the Lustgarten, during a snowstorm, from the roof of a van; a tiny, hatless figure gesticulating above the vast heaving sea of faces and banners. Behind him was the cold façade of the Schloss; and, lining its stone balustrade, the ranks of armed silent police. 'Look at them,' cried Bayer. 'Poor chaps! It seems a shame to make them stand out of doors in weather like this. Never mind; they've got nice thick coats to keep them warm. Who gave them those coats? We did. Wasn't it kind of us? And who's going to give *us* coats? Ask me another.'

'So the old boy's done the trick again,' said Helen Pratt. 'I knew he would. Won ten marks off them at the office, the poor fools.'

It was the Wednesday after the election, and we were standing on the platform of the Zoo Station. Helen had come to see me off in the train to England.

'By the way,' she added, 'what became of that queer card you brought along one evening? Morris, wasn't his name?'

'Norris ... I don't know. I haven't heard from him for ages.'

It was strange that she should have asked that, because I had been thinking about Arthur myself, only a moment before. In my mind, I always connected him with this station. It would soon be six months since he had gone away; it seemed like last week. The moment I got to London, I decided, I would write him a long letter.

CHAPTER NINE

Nevertheless, I didn't write. Why, I hardly know. I was lazy and the weather had turned warm. I thought of Arthur often; so often, indeed, that correspondence seemed unnecessary. It was as though we were in some kind of telepathic communication. Finally, I went away into the country for four months, and discovered, too late, that I'd left the postcard with his address in a drawer somewhere in London. Anyhow, it didn't much matter. He had probably left Paris ages ago by this time. If he wasn't in prison.

At the beginning of October I returned to Berlin. The dear old Tauentzienstrasse hadn't changed. Looking out at it through the taxi window on my way from station, I saw several Nazis in their new S.A. uniforms, now no longer forbidden. They strode along the street very stiff, and were saluted enthusiastically by elderly civilians. Others were posted at street corners, rattling collecting-boxes.

I climbed the familiar staircase. Before I had time to touch the bell, Frl. Schroeder rushed out to greet me with open arms. She must have been watching for my arrival.

'Herr Bradshaw! Herr Bradshaw! Herr Bradshaw! So you've come back to us at last! I declare I must give you a hug! How well you're looking! It hasn't seemed the same since you've been away.'

'How have things been going here, Frl. Schroeder?'

'Well ... I suppose I mustn't complain. In the summer, they were bad. But now ... Come inside, Herr Bradshaw, I've got a surprise for you.'

Gleefully she beckoned me across the hall, flung open the door of the living-room with a dramatic gesture.

'Arthur!'

'My dear William, welcome to Germany!'

'I'd no idea ...'

'Herr Bradshaw, I declare you've grown!'

'Well ... well ... this is indeed a happy reunion. Berlin is herself once more. I propose that we adjourn to my room and drink a glass in celebration of Herr Bradshaw's return. You'll join us, Frl. Schroeder, I hope?'

'Oh ... Most kind of you, Herr Norris, I'm sure.'

'After you.'

'No, please.'

'I couldn't think of it.'

There was a good deal more polite deprecation and bowing before the two of them finally got through the doorway. Familiarity didn't seem to have spoilt their manners. Arthur was as gallant, Frl. Schroeder as coquettish as ever.

The big front bedroom was hardly recognizable. Arthur had moved the bed over into the corner by the window and pushed the sofa nearer to the stove. The stuffy-smelling pots of ferns had disappeared, so had the numerous little crochet mats on the dressing-table, and the metal figures of dogs on the bookcase. The three gorgeously tinted photochromes of bathing nymphs were also missing; in their place I recognized three etchings which had hung in Arthur's dining-room. And, concealing the wash-stand, was a handsome Japanese lacquer screen which used to stand in the hall of the Courbierestrasse flat.

'Flotsam,' Arthur had followed the direction of my glance, 'which I have been able, happily, to save from the wreck.'

'Now, Herr Bradshaw,' put in Frl. Schroeder, 'tell me your candid opinion. Herr Norris will have it that those nymphs were ugly. I always thought them sweetly pretty myself. Of course, I know some people would call them old-fashioned.'

'I shouldn't have said they were ugly,' I replied, diplomatically. 'But it's nice to have a change sometimes, don't you think?'

'Change is the spice of Life,' Arthur murmured, as he fetched glasses from the cupboard. Inside, I caught sight of an array of bottles: 'Which may I offer you, William – kümmel or Benedictine? Frl. Schroeder, I know, prefers cherry brandy.'

Now that I could see the two of them by daylight, I was struck by the contrast. Poor Frl. Schroeder seemed to have got much older; indeed, she was quite an old woman. Her face was pouched and wrinkled with worry, and her skin despite a thick layer of rouge and powder, looked sallow. She hadn't been getting enough to eat. Arthur, on the other hand, looked positively younger. He was fatter in the cheeks and fresh as a rosebud; barbered, manicured and perfumed. He wore a big turquoise ring I hadn't seen before, and an opulent new brown suit. His wig struck a daring, more luxuriant note. It was composed of glossy, waved locks, which wreathed themselves around his temples in tropical abundance. There was something jaunty, even bohemian, in his whole appearance. He might have been a popular actor or a rich violinist.

'How long have you been back here?' I asked.

'Let me see, it must be nearly two months now ... how time flies! I really must apologize for my shortcomings as a correspondent. I've been so very busy; and Frl. Schroeder seemed uncertain of your London address.'

'We're neither of us much good at letter-writing, I'm afraid.'

'The spirit was willing, dear boy. I hope you'll believe that. You were ever-present in my thoughts. It is indeed a pleasure to have you back again. I feel that a load has been lifted from my mind already.'

This sounded rather ominous. Perhaps he was on the rocks again. I only hoped that poor Frl. Schroeder wouldn't have to suffer for it. There she sat, glass in hand, on the sofa, beaming, drinking in every word; her legs were so short that her black velvet shoes dangled an inch above the carpet.

'Just look, Herr Bradshaw,' she extended her wrist, 'what Herr Norris gave me for my birthday. I was so delighted, will you believe me, that I started crying?'

It was a handsome-looking gold bracelet which must have cost at least fifty marks. I was really touched:

'How nice of you, Arthur!'

He blushed. He was quite confused. 'A trifling mark of esteem. I can't tell you what a comfort Frl. Schroeder has been to me. I should like to engage her permanently as my secretary.'

'Oh, Herr Norris, how can you talk such nonsense!'

'I assure you, Frl. Schroeder, I'm quite in earnest.'

'You see how he makes fun of a poor old woman, Herr Bradshaw?'

She was slightly drunk. When Arthur poured her out a second glass of cherry brandy, she upset some of it over her dress. When the commotion which followed this accident had subsided, he said that he must be going out.

'Sorry as I am to break up this festive gathering ... duty calls. Yes, I shall hope to see you this evening, William. Shall we have dinner together? Would that be nice?'

'Very nice.'

'Then I'll say *au revoir*, till eight o'clock.'

I got up to go and unpack. Frl. Schroeder followed me into my room. She insisted on helping me. She was still tipsy and kept putting things into the wrong places; shirts into the drawer of the writing-table, books in the cupboard with the socks. She couldn't stop singing Arthur's praises.

'He came as if Heaven had sent him. I'd got into arrears with the rent, as I haven't done since the inflation days. The porter's wife came up to see me about it several times. "Frl. Schroeder," she said, "we know you and we don't want to be hard on you. But we've all got to live." I declare there were evenings when I was so depressed I'd half a mind to put my head in the oven. And then Herr Norris arrived. I thought he'd just come to pay me a visit, as it were. "How much do you charge for the front bedroom?" he asked. You could have knocked me over with a feather. "Fifty," I said. I didn't dare ask more, with the times so bad. I was trembling all over for fear he'd think it was too much. And what do you think he answered? "Frl. Schroeder," he said, "I couldn't possibly dream of letting you have less than sixty. It would be robbery." I tell you, Herr Bradshaw, I could have kissed his hand.'

Tears stood in Frl. Schroeder's eyes. I was afraid she was going to break down.

'And he pays you regularly?'

'On the moment, Herr Bradshaw. He couldn't be more

punctual if it was you yourself. I've never known anybody to be so particular. Why, do you know, he won't even let me run up a monthly bill for milk? He settles it by the week. "I don't like to feel that I owe anyone a pfennig," he says ... I wish there was more like him.'

That evening, when I suggested eating at the usual restaurant, Arthur, to my surprise, objected:

'It's so noisy there, dear boy. My sensitive nerves revolt against the thought of an evening of jazz. As for the cooking, it is remarkable, even in this benighted town, for its vileness. Let's go to the Montmartre.'

'But, my dear Arthur, it's so terribly expensive.'

'Never mind. Never mind. In this brief life, one cannot always be counting the cost. You're my guest this evening. Let's forget the cares of this harsh world for a few hours and enjoy ourselves.'

'It's very kind of you.'

At the Montmartre, Arthur ordered champagne.

'This is such a peculiarly auspicious event that I feel we may justifiably relax our rigid revolutionary standards.'

I laughed: 'Business seems to be flourishing with you, I must say.'

Arthur squeezed his chin cautiously between finger and thumb.

'I can't complain, William. At the moment. No. But I fear I see breakers ahead.'

'Are you still importing and exporting?'

'Not exactly that ... No ... Well, in a sense, perhaps.'

'Have you been in Paris all this time?'

'More or less. On and off.'

'What were you doing there?'

Arthur glanced uneasily round the luxurious little restaurant; smiled with great charm:

'That's a very leading question, my dear William.'

'Were you working for Bayer?'

'Er – partly. Yes.' A vagueness had come into Arthur's eyes. He was trying to edge away from the subject.

'And you've been seeing him since you got back to Berlin?'

'Of course.' He looked at me with sudden suspicion. 'Why do you ask?'

'I don't know. When I saw you last, you didn't seem very pleased with him, that's all.'

'Bayer and I are on excellent terms.' Arthur spoke with emphasis, paused and added:

'You haven't been telling anybody that I've quarrelled with him, have you?'

'No, of course not, Arthur. Who do you suppose I'd tell?'

Arthur was unmistakably relieved.

'I beg your pardon, William. I might have known that I could rely on your admirable discretion. But if, by any chance, the story were to get about that Bayer and I were not friendly, it might be exceedingly awkward for me, you understand?'

I laughed.

'No, Arthur. I don't understand anything.'

Smiling, Arthur raised his glass.

'Have patience with me, William. You know, I always like to have my little secrets. No doubt the time will come when I shall be able to give you an explanation.'

'Or to invent one.'

'Ha ha. Ha ha. You're as cruel as ever, I see ... which reminds me that I thoughtlessly made an appointment with Anni for ten o'clock ... so that perhaps we ought to be getting on with our dinner.'

'Of course. You mustn't keep her waiting.'

For the rest of the meal Arthur questioned me about London. The cities of Berlin and Paris were tactfully avoided.

Arthur had certainly transformed the daily routine of life at Frl. Schroeder's. Because he insisted on a hot bath every morning, she had to get up an hour earlier, in order to stoke the little old-fashioned boiler. She didn't complain of this. Indeed, she seemed to admire Arthur for the trouble he caused her.

'He's so particular, Herr Bradshaw. More like a lady than a gentleman. Everything in his room has its place, and I get into trouble if it isn't all just as he wants it. I must say, though, it's a pleasure to wait on anybody who takes such care of his things. You ought to see some of his shirts, and his ties.
98

A perfect dream! And his silk underclothes! "Herr Norris," I said to him once, "you should let *me* wear those; they're too fine for a man." I was only joking, of course. Herr Norris does enjoy a joke. He takes in four daily papers, you know, not to mention the weekly illustrateds, and I'm not allowed to throw any of them away. They must all be piled up in their proper order, according to the dates, if you please, on top of the cupboard. It makes me wild, sometimes, when I think of the dust they're collecting. And then, every day, before he goes out, Herr Norris gives me a list as long as your arm of messages I've got to give to people who ring up or call. I have to remember all their names, and which ones he wants to see, and which he doesn't. The door-bell's for ever ringing, nowadays, with telegrams for Herr Norris, and express letters and air mail and I don't know what else. This last fortnight it's been specially bad. If you ask me, I think the ladies are his little weakness.'

'What makes you say that, Frl. Schroeder?'

'Well, I've noticed that Herr Norris is always getting telegrams from Paris. I used to open them, at first, thinking it might be something important which Herr Norris would like to know at once. But I couldn't make head or tail of them. They were all from a lady named Margot. Very affectionate, some of them were, too. "I am sending you a hug," and "last time you forgot to enclose kisses." I must say I should never have the nerve to write such things myself; fancy the clerk at the post office reading them! These French girls must be a shameless lot. From my experience when a woman makes a parade of her feelings like that, she's not worth much ... And then she wrote such a lot of nonsense, besides.'

'What sort of nonsense?'

'Oh, I forget half of it. Stuff about tea-pots and kettles and bread and butter and cake.'

'How very queer.'

'You're right, Herr Bradshaw. It is queer ... I'll tell you what I think.' Frl. Schroeder lowered her voice and glanced towards the door; perhaps she had caught the trick from Arthur. 'I believe it's a kind of secret language. You know? Every word has a double meaning.'

'A code?'

'Yes, that's it.' Frl. Schroeder nodded mysteriously.

'But why should this girl write telegrams to Herr Norris in code, do you suppose? It seems so pointless.'

Frl. Schroeder smiled at my innocence.

'Ah, Herr Bradshaw, you don't know everything, although you're so clever and learned. It takes an old woman like me to understand little mysteries of that sort. It's perfectly plain: this Margot, as she calls herself (I don't suppose it's her real name), must be going to have a baby.'

'And you think that Herr Norris ...'

Frl. Schroeder nodded her head vigorously.

'It's as clear as the nose on your face.'

'Really, I must say, I hardly think ...'

'Oh, it's all very well for you to laugh, Herr Bradshaw, but I'm right, you see if I'm not. After all, Herr Norris is still in the prime of life. I've known gentlemen have families who were old enough to be his father. And, besides, what other reason could she have for writing messages like that?'

'I'm sure I don't know.'

'You see?' cried Frl. Schroeder triumphantly. 'You don't know. Neither do I.'

Every morning Frl. Schroeder would come shuffling through the flat at express speed, like a little steam-engine, screaming:

'Herr Norris! Herr Norris! Your bath is ready! If you don't come quick the boiler will explode!'

'Oh dear!' exclaimed Arthur, in English. 'Just let me clap on my wig.'

He was afraid to go into the bathroom until the water had been turned on and all danger of an explosion was over. Frl. Schroeder would rush in heroically, with face averted and, muffling her hand in a towel, wrench at the hot tap. If the bursting-point was already very near, this would at first emit only clouds of steam, while the water in the boiler boiled with a noise like thunder. Arthur, standing in the doorway, watched Frl. Schroeder's struggles with a nervous, snarling grimace, ready at any moment to bolt for his life.

After the bath came the barber's boy, who was sent up daily from the hairdresser's at the corner to shave Arthur and to comb his wig.

'Even in the wilds of Asia,' Arthur once told me, 'I have never shaved myself when it could possibly be avoided. It's one of those sordid annoying operations which put one in a bad humour for the rest of the day.'

When the barber had gone, Arthur would call to me:

'Come in, dear boy, I'm visible now. Come and talk to me while I powder my nose.'

Seated before the dressing-table in a delicate mauve wrap, Arthur would impart to me the various secrets of his toilet. He was astonishingly fastidious. It was a revelation to me to discover, after all this time, the complex preparations which led up to his every appearance in public. I hadn't dreamed, for example, that he spent ten minutes three times a week in thinning his eyebrows with a pair of pincers. ('Thinning, William; *not* plucking. That's a piece of effeminacy which I abhor.') A massage-roller occupied another fifteen minutes daily of his valuable time; and then there was a thorough manipulation of his cheeks with face cream (seven or eight minutes) and a little judicious powdering (three or four). Pedicure, of course, was an extra; but Arthur usually spent a few moments rubbing ointment on his toes to avert blisters and corns. Nor did he ever neglect a gargle and mouth-wash. ('Coming into daily contact, as I do, with members of the proletariat, I have to defend myself against positive onslaughts of microbes.') All this is not to mention the days on which he actually made up his face. ('I felt I needed a dash of colour this morning; the weather's so depressing.') Or the great fortnightly ablution of his hands and wrists with depilatory lotion. ('I prefer not to be reminded of our kinship with the larger apes.')

After these tedious exertions, it was no wonder that Arthur had a healthy appetite for his breakfast. He had succeeded in coaching Frl. Schroeder as a toast-maker; nor did she once, after the first few days, bring him an unduly hard-boiled egg. He had home-made marmalade, prepared by an English lady who lived in Wilmersdorf and charged nearly double the market price. He used his own special coffee-pot, which he had brought with him from Paris, and drank a special blend of coffee, which had to be sent direct from Hamburg. 'Little things in themselves,' as Arthur said, 'which I have come, through long and painful experience, to value more than many of the over-advertised and overrated luxuries of life.'

At half-past ten he went out, and I seldom saw him again until the evening. I was busy with my teaching. After lunch, he made a habit of coming home and lying down for an hour on his bed. 'Believe me or not, William, I am able to make my mind an absolute blank for whole minutes at a time. It's a matter of practice, of course. Without my siesta, I should quickly become a nervous wreck.'

Three nights a week, Frl. Anni came; and Arthur indulged in his singular pleasures. The noise was perfectly audible in the living-room, where Frl. Schroeder sat sewing.

'Dear, dear!' she said to me once, 'I do hope Herr Norris won't injure himself. He ought to be more careful at his time of life.'

One afternoon, about a week after my arrival, I happened to be in the flat alone. Even Frl. Schroeder had gone out. The door-bell rang. It was a telegram for Arthur, from Paris.

The temptation was simply not to be resisted; I didn't even struggle against it. To make things easier for me, the envelope had not been properly stuck down; it came open in my hand.

'Am very thirsty,' I read, 'hope another kettle will boil soon kisses are for good boys. – Margot.'

I fetched a bottle of glue from my room and fixed the envelope down carefully. Then I left it on Arthur's table and went out to the cinema.

At dinner, that evening, Arthur was visibly depressed. Indeed, he seemed to have no appetite, and sat staring in front of him with a bilious frown.

'What's the matter?' I asked.

'Things in general, dear boy. The state of this wicked world. A touch of *Weltschmerz*, that's all.'

'Cheer up. The course of true love never did run smooth, you know.'

But Arthur didn't react. He didn't even ask me what I meant. Towards the end of our meal, I had to go to the back of the restaurant to make a telephone call. As I returned I saw that he was absorbed in reading a piece of paper which he stuffed hastily into his pocket as I approached. He wasn't quite quick enough. I had recognized the telegram.

CHAPTER TEN

Arthur looked up at me with eyes which were a little too innocent.

'By the way, William,' his tone was carefully casual, 'do you happen to be doing anything next Thursday evening?'

'Nothing that I know of.'

'Excellent. Then may I invite you to a little dinner-party?'

'That sounds very nice. Who else is coming?'

'Oh, it's to be a very small affair. Just ourselves and Baron von Pregnitz.'

Arthur had brought out the name in the most offhand manner possible.

'Kuno!' I exclaimed.

'You seem very surprised, William, not to say displeased.' He was the picture of innocence. 'I always thought you and he were such good friends?'

'So did I, until the last time we met. He practically cut me dead.'

'Oh, my dear boy, if you don't mind my saying so, I think that must have been partly your imagination. I'm sure he'd never do a thing like that; it doesn't sound like him at all.'

'You don't suggest I dreamed it, do you?'

'I'm not doubting your word for an instant, of course. If he was, as you say, a little brusque, I expect he was worried by his many duties. As you probably know, he has a post under the new administration.'

'I think I did read about it in the newspapers, yes.'

'And anyhow, even if he did behave a little strangely on the occasion you mention, I can assure you that he was acting under a misapprehension which has since been removed.'

I smiled.

'You needn't make such a mystery out of it, Arthur. I know half the story already, so you may as well tell me the other half. Your secretary had something to do with it, I think?'

Arthur wrinkled up his nose with a ridiculously fastidious expression.

'Don't call him that, William, please. Just say Schmidt. I don't care to be reminded of the association. Those who are foolish enough to keep snakes as pets usually have cause to regret it, sooner or later.'

'All right, then. Schmidt ... Go on.'

'I see that, as usual, you're better informed than I'd supposed,' Arthur sighed. 'Well, well, if you want to hear the whole melancholy truth, you must, painful as it is for me to dwell on. As you know, my last weeks at the Courbierestrasse were spent in a state of excruciating financial anxiety.'

'I do indeed.'

'Well, without going into a lot of sordid details which are neither here nor there, I was compelled to try and raise money. I cast about in all sorts of likely and unlikely directions. And, as a last desperate resort when the wolf was literally scratching at the door, I put my pride in my pocket ...'

'And asked Kuno to lend you some?'

'Thank you, dear boy. With your customary consideration for my feelings, you help me over the most painful part of the story ... Yes, I sank so low. I violated one of my most sacred principles – never to borrow from a friend. (For I may say I did regard him as a friend, a dear friend.) Yes ...'

'And he refused? The stingy brute!'

'No, William. There you go too fast. You misjudge him. I have no reason to suppose that he would have refused. Quite the contrary. This was the first time I had ever approached him. But Schmidt got to know of my intentions. I can only suppose he had been systematically opening all my letters. At any rate, he went straight to Pregnitz and advised him not to advance me the money; giving all sorts of reasons, most of which were the most monstrous slanders. Despite all my long experience of human nature, I should hardly have believed such treachery and ingratitude possible ...

'Whatever made him do it?'

'Chiefly, I think, pure spite. As far as one can follow the workings of his foul mind. But, undoubtedly, the creature was also afraid that, in this case, he would be deprived of his pound of flesh. He usually arranged these loans himself, you know, and subtracted a percentage before handing over the money at all ... It humbles me to the earth to have to tell you this.'

'And I suppose he was right? I mean, you weren't going to give him any, this time, were you?'

'Well, no. After his villainous behaviour over the sitting-room carpet, it was hardly to be expected that I should. You remember the carpet?'

'I should think I did.'

'The carpet incident was, so to speak, the declaration of war between us. Although I still endeavoured to meet his demands with the utmost fairness.'

'And what did Kuno have to say to all this?'

'He was, naturally, most upset, and indignant. And, I must add, rather unnecessarily unkind. He wrote me a most unpleasant letter. Quite gentlemanly, of course; he is always that. But frigid. Very frigid.'

'I'm surprised that he took Schmidt's word against yours.'

'No doubt Schmidt had ways and means of convincing him. There are some incidents in my career, as you doubtless know, which are very easily capable of misinterpretation.'

'And he brought me into it, as well?'

'I regret to say that he did. That pains me more than anything else in the whole affair; to think that you should have been dragged down into the mud in which I was already wallowing.'

'What exactly did he tell Kuno about me?'

'He seems to have suggested, not to put too fine a point upon it, that you were an accomplice in my nefarious crimes.'

'Well I'm damned.'

'I need hardly add that he painted us both as Bolsheviks of the deepest crimson.'

'He flattered me there, I'm afraid.'

'Well – er – yes. That's one way of looking at it, of course. Unfortunately, revolutionary ardour is no recommendation to the Baron's favour. His view of the members of the Left Wing is somewhat primitive. He imagines us with pockets full of bombs.'

'And yet, in spite of all this, he's ready to have dinner with us next Thursday?'

'Oh, our relations are very different now, I'm glad to say. I've seen him several times since my return to Berlin. Considerable diplomacy was required, of course; but I think I've more or less convinced him of the absurdity of Schmidt's accusation. By a piece of good luck, I was able to be of service in a little matter. Pregnitz is essentially a reasonable man; he's always open to conviction.'

I smiled: 'You seem to have put yourself to a good deal of trouble on his account. I hope it'll prove to have been worth while.'

'One of my characteristics, William, you may call it a weakness if you like, is that I can never bear to lose a friend, if it can possibly be avoided.'

'And you're anxious that I shan't lose a friend either?'

'Well, yes, I must say, if I thought I had been the cause, even indirectly, of a permanent estrangement between Pregnitz and yourself, it would make me very unhappy. If any little doubts or resentments do still exist on either side, I sincerely hope that this meeting will put an end to them.'

'There's no ill feeling as far as I'm concerned.'

'I'm glad to hear you say that, dear boy. Very glad. It's so stupid to bear grudges. In this life one's apt to lose a great deal through a mistaken sense of pride.'

'A great deal of money, certainly.'

'Yes ... that too.' Arthur pinched his chin and looked thoughtful. 'Although I was speaking, just then, more from the spiritual point of view than the material.'

His tone implied a gentle rebuke.

'By the way,' I asked, 'what's Schmidt doing now?'

'My dear William,' Arthur looked pained, 'how in the world should I know?'

'I thought he might have been bothering you.'

'During my first month in Paris, he wrote me a number of letters full of the most preposterous threats and demands for money. I simply disregarded them. Since then, I've heard nothing more.'

'He's never turned up at Frl. Schroeder's?'

'Thank God, no. Not up to now. It's one of my nightmares that he'll somehow discover the address.'

'I suppose he's more or less bound to, sooner or later?'

'Don't say that, William. Don't say that, please ... I have enough to worry me as it is. The cup of my afflictions would indeed be full.'

As we walked to the restaurant on the evening of the dinner-party, Arthur primed me with final instructions.

'You will be most careful, won't you, dear boy, not to let drop any reference to Bayer or to our political beliefs?'

'I'm not completely mad.'

'Of course not, William. Please don't think I meant anything offensive. But even the most cautious of us betray ourselves at times ... Just one other little point: perhaps, at this stage of the proceedings, it would be more politic not to address Pregnitz by his Christian name. It's as well to preserve one's distance. That sort of thing's so easily misunderstood.'

'Don't you worry. I'll be as stiff as a poker.'

'Not stiff, dear boy, I do beg. Perfectly easy, perfectly natural. A shade formal, perhaps, just at first. Let him make the advances. A little polite reserve, that's all.'

'If you go on much longer, you'll get me into such a state that I shan't be able to open my mouth.'

We arrived at the restaurant to find Kuno already seated at the table Arthur had reserved. The cigarette between his fingers was burnt down almost to the end; his face wore an expression of well-bred boredom. At the sight of him, Arthur positively gasped with horror.

'My dear Baron, do forgive me, please. I wouldn't have had this happen for the world. Did I say half past? I did? And you've been waiting a quarter of an hour? You overwhelm me with shame. Really, I don't know how to apologize enough.'

Arthur's fulsomeness seemed to embarrass the Baron as much as it did myself. He made a faint, distasteful gesture with his fin-like hand and murmured something which I couldn't hear.

'... too stupid of me. I simply can't conceive how I can have been so foolish ...'

We all sat down. Arthur prattled on and on; his apologies developed like an air with variations. He blamed his memory and recalled other instances when it had failed him. ('I'm reminded of a most unfortunate occasion in Washington on which I entirely forgot to attend an important diplomatic function at the house of the Spanish Ambassador.') He found fault with his watch; lately, he told us, it had been gaining. ('I usually make a point, about this time of year, of sending it to the makers in Zürich to be overhauled.') And he assured the Baron, at least five times, that I had no responsibility whatever for the mistake. I wished I could sink through the floor. Arthur, I could see, was nervous and unsure of himself; the variations wavered uneasily and threatened, at every moment, to collapse into discords. I had seldom known him to be so verbose and never so boring. Kuno had retired behind his monocle. His face was as discreet as the menu, and as unintelligible.

By the middle of the fish, Arthur had talked himself out. A silence followed which was even more uncomfortable than his chatter. We sat round the elegant little dinner-table like three people absorbed in a difficult chess problem. Arthur manipulated his chin and cast furtive, despairing glances in my direction, signalling for help. I declined to respond. I was sulky and resentful. I'd come here this evening on the understanding that Arthur had already more or less patched things up with Kuno; that the way was paved to a general reconciliation. Nothing of the kind. Kuno was still suspicious of Arthur, and no wonder, considering the way he was behaving now. I felt his eye questioningly upon me from time to time and went on eating, looking neither to right nor to left.

'Mr Bradshaw's just returned from England.' It was as though Arthur had given me a violent push into the middle of the stage. His tone implored me to play my part. They were both looking at me, now. Kuno was interested but cautious; Arthur frankly abject. They were so funny in their different ways that I had to smile.

'Yes,' I said, 'at the beginning of the month.'

'Excuse me, you were in London?'

'Part of the time, yes.'

'Indeed?' Kuno's eye lit up with a tender gleam. 'And how was it there, may I ask?'

'We had lovely weather in September.'

'Yes, I see ...' A faint, fishy smile played over his lips; he seemed to savour delicious memories. His monocle shone with a dreamy light. His distinguished, preserved profile became pensive and maudlin and sad.

'I shall always maintain,' put in the incorrigible Arthur, 'that London in September has a charm all its own. I remember one exceptionally beautiful autumn – in nineteen hundred and four, I think it was. Or possibly nineteen hundred and five. I used to stroll down to Waterloo Bridge before breakfast and admire St Paul's. At that time, I had a suite at the Savoy Hotel ...'

Kuno appeared not to have heard him.

'And, excuse me, how are the Horse Guards?'

'Still sitting there.'

'Yes? I am glad to hear this, you see. Very glad ...'

I grinned. Kuno smiled, fishy and subtle. Arthur uttered a surprisingly coarse snigger which he instantly checked with his hand. Then Kuno threw back his head and laughed out loud: 'Ho! Ho! Ho!' I had never heard him really laugh before. His laugh was a curiosity, an heirloom; something handed down from the dinner-tables of the last century; aristocratic, manly and sham, scarcely to be heard nowadays except on the legitimate stage. He seemed a little ashamed of it himself, for, recovering, he added, in a tone of apology:

'You see, excuse me, I can remember them very well.'

'I'm reminded,' Arthur leaned forward across the table; his tone became spicy, 'of a story which used to be told about a certain peer of the realm ... let's call him Lord X. I can vouch for it, because I met him once in Cairo, a most eccentric man ...'

There was no doubt about it, the party had been saved. I began to breathe more freely. Kuno relaxed by imperceptible stages, from polite suspicion to positive jollity. Arthur, recovering his nerve, was naughty and funny. We drank a good deal of brandy and three whole bottles of Pommard. I told an extremely stupid story about the two Scotsmen who went into a synagogue. Kuno started to nudge me with his foot. In an absurdly short space of time I looked at the clock and saw it was eleven.

'Good gracious!' exclaimed Arthur. 'If you'll forgive me, I must fly. A little engagement ...'

I looked at Arthur questioningly. I had never known him to make appointments at this hour of the night; besides, it wasn't Anni's evening. Kuno didn't seem at all put out, however. He was most gracious.

'Don't mention it, my dear fellow ... We quite understand.' His foot pressed mine under the table.

'You know,' I said, when Arthur had left us, 'I really ought to be getting home, too.'

'Oh, surely not.'

'I think so,' I said firmly, smiling and moving my foot away. He was squeezing a corn.

'You see, I should like so very much to show you my new flat. We can be there in the car in ten minutes.'

'I should love to see it; some other time.'

He smiled faintly.

'Then may I, perhaps, give you a lift home?'

'Thank you very much.'

The remarkably handsome chauffeur saluted pertly, tucked us into the depths of the vast black limousine. As we slid forward along the Kurfürstendamm, Kuno took my hand under the fur rug.

'You're still angry with me,' he murmured reproachfully.

'Why should I be?'

'Oh yes, excuse me, you are.'

'Really, I'm not.'

Kuno gave my hand a limp squeeze.

'May I ask you something?'

'Ask away.'

'You see, I don't wish to be personal. Do you believe in Platonic friendship?'

'I expect so,' I said, guardedly.

The answer seemed to satisfy him. His tone became more confidential: 'You're sure you won't come up and see my flat? Not for five minutes?'

'Not tonight.'

'Quite sure?' He squeezed.

'Quite, quite sure.'

'Some other evening?' Another squeeze.

I laughed: 'I think I should see it better in the daytime, shouldn't I?'

Kuno sighed gently, but did not pursue the subject. A few moments later, the limousine stopped outside my door. Glancing up at Arthur's window, I saw that the light was burning. I didn't remark on this to Kuno, however.

'Well, good night, and thank you for the lift.'

'Do not mention it, please.'

I nodded towards the chauffeur: 'Shall I tell him to take you home?'

'No, thank you,' Kuno spoke rather sadly, but with an attempt at a smile. 'I'm afraid not. Not just yet.'

He sank back upon the cushions, the smile still frozen on his face, his monocle catching a ghostly glassy gleam from the street lamp as he was driven away.

As I entered the flat, Arthur appeared, in shirt-sleeves, at his bedroom doorway. He seemed rather perturbed.

'Back already, William?'

I grinned: 'Aren't you pleased to see me, Arthur?'

'Of course, dear boy. What a question! I didn't expect you quite so soon, that's all.'

'I know you didn't. Your appointment doesn't seem to have kept you very long, either.'

'It – er – fell through.' Arthur yawned. He was too sleepy even to tell lies.

I laughed: 'You meant well, I know. Don't worry. We parted on the best of terms.'

He brightened at once: 'You did? Oh, I'm so very glad. For the moment, I was afraid some little hitch might have occurred. Now I can go to sleep with a mind relieved. Once again, William, I must thank you for your invaluable support.'

'Always glad to oblige,' I said. 'Good night.'

CHAPTER ELEVEN

The first week in November came and the traffic strike was declared. It was ghastly, sopping weather. Everything out of doors was covered with a layer of greasy, fallen dirt. A few trams were running, policemen posted fore and aft. Some of these were attacked, the windows smashed and the passengers forced to get out. The streets were deserted, wet, raw and grey. Von Papen's Government was expected to proclaim martial law. Berlin seemed profoundly indifferent. Proclamations, shootings, arrests; they were all nothing new. Helen Pratt was putting her money on Schleicher: 'He's the foxiest of the lot,' she told me. 'Look here, Bill, I'll bet you five marks he's in before Christmas. Like to take me on?' I declined.

Hitler's negotiations with the Right had broken down; the Hakenkreuz was even flirting mildly with the Hammer and Sickle. Telephone conversations, so Arthur told me, had already taken place between the enemy camps. Nazi stormtroopers joined with communists in the crowds which jeered at the blacklegs and pelted them with stones. Meanwhile, on the soaked advertisement pillars, Nazi posters represented the K.P.D. as a bogy skeleton in Red Army uniform. In a few days there would be another election; our fourth this year. Political meetings were well attended; they were cheaper than going to the movies or getting drunk. Elderly people sat indoors, in the damp, shabby houses, brewing malt coffee or weak tea and talking without animation of the Smash.

On November 7th, the election results were out. The Nazis had lost two million votes. The Communists had gained eleven seats. They had a majority of over 100,000 in Berlin. 'You see,' I told Frl. Schroeder, 'it's all your doing.' We had persuaded her to go down to the beer-shop at the corner and vote, for the first time in her life. And now she was as delighted as if she'd backed a winner: 'Herr Norris! Herr Norris! Only think! I did just what you told me; and it's all come out as you said! The porter's wife's ever so cross. She's followed the elections for years, and she would have it that the Nazis were going to win another million this time. I had a good laugh at her, I can tell you. "Aha, Frau Schneider!" I said to her, "I understand something about politics, too, you see!"'

During the morning, Arthur and I went round to the Wilhelmstrasse, to Bayer's office, 'for a little taste,' as he put it, 'of the fruits of victory.' Several hundred others seemed to have had the same idea. There was such a crowd of people coming and going on the stairs that we had difficulty in getting into the building at all. Everybody was in the best of spirits, shouting to each other, greeting, whistling, singing. As we struggled upwards, we met Otto on his way down. He nearly wrung my hand off in excitement.

'*Mensch!* Willi! *Jetzt geht's los!* Just let them talk about forbidding the Party now! If they do, we'll fight! The old Nazis are done for, that's certain. In six months, Hitler won't have any storm-troops left!'

Half a dozen of his friends were with him. They all shook my hand with the warmth of long-lost brothers. Meanwhile, Otto had flung himself upon Arthur like a young bear. 'What, Arthur, you old sow, you here too? Isn't it fine? Isn't it grand? Why, I'm so pleased I could knock you into the middle of next week!'

He dealt Arthur an affectionate hook in the ribs which made him squirm. Several of the bystanders laughed sympathetically. 'Good old Arthur!' exclaimed one of Otto's friends loudly. The name was overheard, taken up, passed from mouth to mouth. 'Arthur . . . who's Arthur? Why, man, don't you know who Arthur is?' No, they didn't know. Equally, they didn't care. It was a name, a focus-point for the enthusiasm of all these excited young people; it served its purpose. 'Arthur! Arthur!' was caught up on all sides. People were shouting it on the floor above us; in the hallway below. 'Arthur's here!' 'Arthur for ever!' 'We want Arthur!' The storm of voices had risen in a moment. A mighty cheer, exuberant, half-humorous, burst spontaneously from a hundred throats. Another followed it, and another. The crazy old staircase shook; a tiny flake of plaster was dislodged from the ceiling. In this confined space, the reverberation was terrific; the crowd was excited to find what a noise it could make. There was a powerful, convulsive, surging movement inwards, towards the unseen object of admiration. A wave of admirers elbowed their way up the stairs, to collide with another wave, cascading down from above. Everybody wanted to touch Arthur. A rain of hand-claps descended on his wincing shoulders. An ill-timed attempt to hoist him into the air nearly resulted in his being pitched headlong over the banisters. His hat had been knocked off. I had managed to save it and was fully expecting to have to rescue his wig as well. Gasping for breath, Arthur tried, in a muddled way, to rise to the occasion; 'Thank you ...' he managed to articulate. 'Most kind ... really don't deserve ... good gracious! Oh dear!'

He might have been quite seriously injured, had not Otto and his friends forced a way for him to the top of the staircase. We scrambled in the wake of their powerful, barging bodies. Arthur clutched my arm, half scared, half shyly pleased. 'Fancy their knowing me, William,' he panted into my ear.

But the crowd hadn't done with him yet. Now that we had reached the office door, we occupied a position of vantage and could be seen by the mass of struggling people wedged in the staircase below. At the sight of Arthur, another terrific cheer shook the building. 'Speech!' yelled somebody. And the cry was echoed: 'Speech! Speech! Speech!' Those on the stairs began a rhythmical stamping and shouting; the heavy tread of their boots was as formidable as the stroke of a giant piston. If Arthur didn't do something to stop it, it seemed probable that the entire staircase would collapse.

At this critical moment, the door of the office opened. It was Bayer himself, come out to see what all the noise was about. His smiling eyes took in the scene with the amusement of a tolerant schoolmaster. The uproar did not disconcert him in the least; he was used to it. Smiling, he shook hands with the scared and embarrassed Arthur, laying a reassuring hand upon his shoulder. 'Ludwig!' roared the on-lookers. 'Ludwig! Arthur! Speech!' Bayer laughed at them and made a good-humoured gesture of salute and dismissal. Then he turned, escorting Arthur and myself into the office. The noise outside gradually subsided into singing and shouted jokes. In the outer office the typists were doing their best to carry on work amidst groups of eagerly arguing men and women. The walls were plastered with news-sheets displaying the election results. We elbowed our way into Bayer's little room. Arthur sank at once into a chair and began fanning himself with his recovered hat.

'Well, well ... dear me! I feel quite carried away, as it were, in the whirl of history; distinctly battered. This is indeed a red-letter day for the Cause.'

Bayer's eyes regarded him with vivid, faintly amused interest.

'It surprises you, eh?'

'Well – er – I must admit that hardly, in my most sanguine dreams, had I dared to expect such a very decisive – er – victory.'

Bayer nodded encouragingly.

'It is good, yes. But it will be unwise, I think, to exaggerate the importances of this success. Many factors have contributed to it. It is, how do you call, symptomic?'

'Symptomatic,' Arthur corrected, with a little cough. His blue eyes shifted uneasily over the litter of papers on Bayer's writing-table. Bayer gave him a brilliant smile.

'Ah, yes. Symptomatic. It is symptomatic of the phase through which we are at present passing. We are not yet ready to cross the Wilhelmstrasse.' He made a humorous gesture of his hand, indicating, through the window, the direction of the Foreign Office and Hindenburg's residence. 'No. Not quite yet.'

'Do you think,' I asked, 'that this means the Nazis are done for?'

He shook his head with decision. 'Unfortunately, no. We may not be so optimistic. This reverse is for them of a temporary character only. You see, Mr Bradshaw, the economic situation is in their favour. We shall hear much more of our friends, I think.'

'Oh, please don't say anything so unpleasant,' murmured Arthur, fidgeting with his hat. His eyes continued furtively to explore the writing table. Bayer's glance followed them.

'You do not like the Nazis, eh, Norris?'

His tone was rich with amusement. He appeared to find Arthur extremely funny at this precise moment. I was at a loss to understand why. Moving over to the table, he began, as if abstractedly, to handle the papers which lay there.

'Really!' protested Arthur, in shocked tones. 'How can you ask? Naturally, I dislike them. Odious creatures ...'

'Ah, but you should not!' With great deliberation, Bayer took a key from his pocket, unlocked a drawer in the writing-table, and drew from it a heavy sealed packet. His red-brown eyes sparkled teasingly. 'This outlook is quite false. The Nazi of today can be the communist of tomorrow. When they have seen where their leaders' programme has brought them, they may not be so very difficult to convince. I wish all opposition could be thus overcome. There are others, you see, who will not listen to such arguments.'

Smiling, he turned the packet in his hands. Arthur's eyes were fastened upon it, as if in unwilling fascination; Bayer seemed to be amusing himself by exerting his hypnotic powers. At all events, Arthur was plainly most uncomfortable.

'Er – yes. Well ... you may be right ...'

There was a curious silence. Bayer was smiling to himself, subtly, with the corners of his lips. I had never seen him in this mood before. Suddenly, he appeared to become aware of what he was holding.

'Why, of course, my dear Norris ... These are the documents I had promised to show you. Can you be so kind as to let me have them tomorrow again? We have to forward them, you know, as quickly as possible.'

'Certainly. Of course ...' Arthur had fairly jumped out of his seat to receive the packet. He was like a dog which has been put on trust for a lump of sugar. 'I'll take the greatest care of them, I assure you.'

Bayer smiled, but said nothing.

Some minutes later, he escorted us affably out of the premises by the back staircase which led down into the courtyard. Arthur thus avoided another encounter with his admirers.

As we walked away along the street, he seemed thoughtful and vaguely unhappy. Twice he sighed.

'Feeling tired?' I asked.

'Not tired, dear boy. No ... I was merely indulging in my favourite vice of philosophizing. When you get to my age you'll see more and more clearly how very strange and complex life is. Take this morning, for instance. The simple enthusiasm of all those young people; it touched me very deeply. On such occasions, one feels oneself so unworthy. I suppose there are individuals who do not suffer from a conscience. But I am not one of them.'

The strangest thing about this odd outburst was that Arthur obviously meant what he said. It was a genuine fragment of a confession, but I could make nothing of it.

'Yes,' I encouraged experimentally, 'I sometimes feel like that myself.'

Arthur didn't respond. He merely sighed for the third time. A sudden shadow of anxiety passed over his face; hastily he fingered the bulge in his pocket made by the papers which Bayer had given him. They were still there. He breathed relief.

November passed without much event. I had more pupils again, and was busy. Bayer gave me two long manuscripts to translate.

There were rumours that the K.P.D. would be forbidden; soon, in a few weeks. Otto was scornful. The Government would never dare, he said. The Party would fight. All the members of his cell had revolvers. They hung them, he told me, by strings from the bars of a cellar-grating in their *Lokal*, so that the police shouldn't find them. The police were very active these days. Berlin, we heard, was to be cleaned up. Plain-clothes men had paid several unexpected calls on Olga, but had failed, so far, to find anything. She was being very careful.

We dined with Kuno several times and had tea at his flat. He was sentimental and preoccupied by turns. The intrigues which were going on within the Cabinet probably caused him a good deal of worry. And he regretted the freedom of his earlier bohemian existence. His public responsibilities debarred him from the society of the young men I had met at his Mecklenburg villa. Only their photographs remained to console him now, bound in a sumptuous album which he kept locked away in an obscure cupboard. Kuno showed it to me one day when we were alone.

'Sometimes in the evenings, I like to look at them, you see? And then I make up a story to myself that we are all living together on a deserted island in the Pacific Ocean. Excuse me, you don't think this very silly, I hope?'

'Not at all,' I assured him.

'You see, I knew you'd understand.' Encouraged, he proceeded shyly to further confessions. The desert island fantasy was nothing new. He had been cherishing it for months already; it had developed gradually into a private cult. Under its influence he had acquired a small library of stories for boys, most of them in English, which dealt with this particular kind of adventure. He had told his bookseller that he wanted them for a nephew in London. Kuno had found most of the books subtly unsatisfactory. There had been grown-ups in them, or buried treasures, or marvellous scientific inventions. He had no use for any of these. Only one story had really pleased him. It was called *The Seven Who Got Lost*.

'This is the work of genius, I find.' Kuno was quite in earnest. His eyes gleamed with enthusiasm. 'I should be so very happy if you would care to read it, you see?'

I took the book home. It was certainly not at all bad of its kind. Seven boys, of ages ranging from sixteen to nineteen, are washed ashore on an uninhabited island, where there is water and plenty of vegetation. They have no food with them and no tools but a broken penknife. The book was a matter-of-fact account, cribbed largely from the *Swiss Family Robinson*, of how they hunted, fished, built a hut and finally got themselves rescued. I read it at a sitting and brought it back to Kuno next day. He was delighted when I praised it.

'You remember Jack?'

'The one who was so good at fishing? Yes.'

'Now tell me, please, is he not like Günther?'

I had no idea who Günther was, but rightly guessed him to have been one of the Mecklenburg house-party.

'Yes, he is rather.'

'Oh, I am so glad you find this, too. And Tony?'

'The one who was such a marvellous climber?'

Kuno nodded eagerly: 'Doesn't he remind you of Heinz?'

'I see what you mean.'

In this way we worked through the other characters, Teddy, Bob, Rex, Dick: Kuno supplied a counterpart to each. I congratulated myself on having really read the book and being thus able to pass this curious examination with credit. Last of all came Jimmy, the hero, the champion swimmer, the boy who always led the others in an emergency and had a brain-wave to solve every difficulty.

'You didn't recognize him, perhaps?'

Kuno's tone was oddly, ludicrously coy. I saw that I must beware of giving the wrong answer. But what on earth was I to say?

'I did have some idea ...' I ventured.

'You did?' He was actually blushing.

I nodded, smiling, trying to look intelligent, waiting for a hint.

'He is myself, you see.' Kuno had the simplicity of complete conviction. 'When I was a boy. But exactly ... This writer is a genius. He tells things about me which nobody else can know. I am Jimmy. Jimmy is myself. It is marvellous.'

'It's certainly very strange,' I agreed.

After this, we had several talks about the island. Kuno told me exactly how he pictured it, and dwelt in detail upon the appearance and characteristics of his various imaginary companions. He certainly had a most vivid imagination. I wished that the author of *The Seven Who Got Lost* could have been there to hear him. He would have been startled to behold the exotic fruit of his unambitious labours. I gathered that I was Kuno's only confidant on the subject. I felt as embarrassed as some unfortunate person who has been forcibly made a member of a secret society. If Arthur was with us, Kuno showed only too plainly his desire to get rid of him and be alone with me. Arthur noticed this, of course, and irritated me by putting the obvious construction on our private interviews. All the same, I hadn't the heart to give Kuno's poor little mystery away.

'Look here,' I said to him once, 'why don't you do it?'

'Please?'

'Why don't you clear out to the Pacific and find an island like the one in the book, and really live there? Other people have done it. There's absolutely no reason why you shouldn't.'

Kuno shook his head sadly.

'Excuse me, no. It's impossible.'

His tone was so final and so sad that I was silent. Nor did I ever make such a suggestion to him again.

As the month advanced, Arthur became increasingly depressed. I soon noticed that he had less money than formerly. Not that he complained. Indeed, he had become most secretive about his troubles. He made his economies as unobtrusively as possible, giving up taxis on the ground that a bus was just as quick, avoiding the expensive restaurants because, as he said, rich food disagreed with his digestion. Anni's visits were less frequent also. Arthur had taken to going to bed early. During the day, he was out more than ever. He spent a good deal of his time, I discovered, in Bayer's office.

It wasn't long before another telegram arrived from Paris. I had no difficulty in persuading Frl. Schroeder, whose curiosity was as shameless as my own, to steam open the envelope before Arthur's return for his afternoon nap. With heads pressed close together, we read:

Tea you sent no good at all cannot understand why believe you have another girl no kisses.

Margot.

'You see,' exclaimed Frl. Schroeder, in delighted horror, 'she's been trying to stop it.'

'What on earth ..,'

'Why, Herr Bradshaw,' in her impatience she gave my hand a little slap, 'how can you be so dense! The baby, of course. He must have sent her some stuff ... Oh, these men! If he'd only come to me, I could have told him what to do. It never fails.'

'For Heaven's sake, Frl. Schroeder, don't say anything about this to Herr Norris.'

'Oh, Herr Bradshaw, you can trust me!'

I think, all the same, that her manner must have given Arthur some hint of what we had done. For, after this, the French telegrams ceased to arrive. Arthur, I supposed, had prudently arranged to have them delivered to some other address.

And then one evening early in December, when Arthur was out and Frl. Schroeder was having a bath, the door-bell rang. I answered it myself. There, on the threshold, stood Schmidt.

'Good evening, Mr Bradshaw.'

He looked shabby and unkempt. His great, greasy moon-face was unwholesomely white. At first I thought he must be drunk.

'What do you want?' I asked.

Schmidt grinned unpleasantly. 'I want to see Norris.' He must have read what was in my mind, for he added: 'You needn't bother to tell me any lies, because I know he's living here, now, see?'

'Well, you can't see him now. He's gone out.'

'Are you sure he's out?' Schmidt regarded me smiling, through half-closed eyes.

'Perfectly. Otherwise I shouldn't have told you so.'

'So ... I see.'

We stood looking at each other for some moments, smiling with dislike. I was tempted to slam the door in his face.

'Mr Norris would do better to see me,' said Schmidt, after a pause, in an offhand, casual tone, as though this were his first mention of the subject. I put the side of my foot as unostentatiously as possible against the door, in case he should suddenly turn rough.

'I think,' I said gently, 'that that's a matter for Mr Norris himself to judge.'

'Won't you tell him I'm here?' Schmidt glanced down at my·foot and impudently grinned. Our voices were so mild and low-pitched that anybody passing up the staircase would have supposed us to be two neighbours, engaged in a friendly chat.

'I've told you once already that Mr Norris isn't at home. Don't you understand German?'

Schmidt's smile was extraordinarily insulting. His half-closed eyes regarded me with a certain amusement, a qualified disapproval, as though I were a picture badly out of drawing. He spoke slowly, with elaborate patience.

'Perhaps it wouldn't be troubling you too much to give Mr Norris a message from me?'

'Yes. I'll do that.'

'Will you be so kind as to tell Mr Norris that I'll wait another three days, but no longer? You understand? At the end of this week, if I haven't heard from him, I shall do what I said in my letter. He'll know what I mean. He thinks I daren't, perhaps. Well, he'll soon find out what a mistake he's made. I don't want trouble, unless he asks for it. But I've got to live ... I've got to look after myself the same as he has. I mean to have my rights. He needn't think he can keep me down in the gutter ...'

He was actually trembling all over. Some violent emotion, rage or extreme weakness, was shaking his body like a leaf. I thought for a moment that he would fall.

'Are you ill?' I asked.

My question had an extraordinary effect on Schmidt. His oily, smiling sneer stiffened into a tense mask of hatred. He had utterly lost control of himself. Coming a step nearer to me, he literally shouted in my face:

'It isn't any business of yours, do you hear? Just you tell Norris what I said. If he doesn't do what I want, I'll make him sorry for the day he was born! And you too, you swine!'

His hysterical fury infected me suddenly. Stepping back, I

flung the door to with a violent slam, hoping to catch his thrust-forward, screaming face on the point of the jaw. But there was no impact. His voice stopped like a gramophone from which the needle is lifted. Nor did he utter another sound. As I stood there behind the closed door, my heart pounding with anger, I heard his light footsteps cross the landing and begin to descend the stairs.

CHAPTER TWELVE

An hour later, Arthur returned home. I followed him into his room to break the news.

'Schmidt's been here.'

If Arthur's wig had been suddenly jerked from his head by a fisherman, he could hardly have looked more startled.

'William, please tell me the worst at once. Don't keep me in suspense. What time was this? Did you see him yourself? What did he say?'

'He's trying to blackmail you, isn't he?'

Arthur looked at me quickly.

'Did he admit that?'

'He as good as told me. He says he's written to you already, and that if you don't do what he wants by the end of the week there'll be trouble.'

'He actually said that? Oh dear ...'

'You should have told me he'd written,' I said reproachfully.

'I know, dear boy, I know ...' Arthur was the picture of distress. 'It's been on the tip of my tongue several times this last fortnight. But I didn't want to worry you unnecessarily. I kept hoping that, somehow, it might all blow over.'

'Now, look here, Arthur; the point is this: does Schmidt really know anything about you which can do you harm?'

He had been nervously pacing the room, and now sank, a disconsolate shirt-sleeved figure, into a chair, forlornly regarding his button-boots.

'Yes, William.' His voice was small and apologetic. 'I'm afraid he does.'

'What sort of things does he know?'

'Really, I ... I don't think, even for you, that I can go into the details of my hideous past.'

'I don't want details. What I want to know is, could Schmidt get you involved in any kind of criminal charge?'

Arthur considered this for some moments, thoughtfully rubbing his chin.

'I don't think he dare try it. No.'

'I'm not so sure,' I said. 'He seemed to me to be in a pretty bad way. Desperate enough for anything. He looked as though he wasn't getting much to eat.'

Arthur stood up again and began walking about the room, rapidly, with small anxious steps.

'Let's keep quite calm, William. Let's think this out together quietly.'

'Do you think, from your experience of Schmidt, that he'd keep quiet if you paid him a lump sum down to leave you alone?'

Arthur did not hesitate:

'I'm quite sure he wouldn't. It would merely whet his appetite for my blood ... Oh dear, oh dear!'

'Suppose you left Germany altogether? Would he be able to get at you then?'

Arthur stopped short in the middle of a gesture of extreme agitation.

'No, I suppose ... that is, no, quite definitely not.' He regarded me with dismay. 'You aren't suggesting I should do that, I hope?'

'It seems drastic. But what's the alternative?'

'I see none. Certainly.'

'Neither do I.'

Arthur moved his shoulders in a shrug of despair.

'Yes, yes, my dear boy. It's easy enough to say that. But where's the money coming from?'

'I thought you were pretty well off now?' I pretended mild surprise. Arthur's glance slid away, evasively, from beneath my own.

'Only under certain conditions.'

'You mean, you can only earn money here?'

'Well, chiefly ...' He didn't like this catechism, and began to fidget. I could no longer resist trying a shot in the dark.

'But you get paid from Paris?'

I had scored a bull. Arthur's dishonest blue eyes showed

a startled flicker, but no more. Perhaps he wasn't altogether unprepared for the question.

'My dear William, I haven't the least idea what you're talking about.'

I grinned.

'Never mind, Arthur. It's no business of mine. I only want to help you, if I can.'

'It's most kind of you, dear boy, I'm sure.' Arthur sighed. 'This is all most difficult; most complicated ...'

'Well, we've got one point clear, at any rate ... Now, the best thing you can do is to send Schmidt some money at once, to keep him quiet. How much did he ask for?'

'A hundred down,' said Arthur in a subdued voice, 'and then fifty a week.'

'I must say he's got a nerve. Could you manage a hundred and fifty, do you think?'

'At a pinch, I suppose, yes. It goes against the grain.'

'I know. But this'll save you ten times as much in the end. Now what I suggest is, you send him the hundred and fifty, with a letter promising him the balance on the first of January ...'

'Really, William ...'

'Wait a minute. And meanwhile, you'll arrange to be out of Germany before the end of December. That gives you three weeks' grace. If you pay up meekly now, he won't bother you again till then. He'll think he's got you in his pocket.'

'Yes. I suppose you're right. I shall have to accustom myself to the idea. All this is so sudden.' Arthur had a momentary flare-up of resentment. 'That odious serpent! If ever I find an opportunity of dealing with him once for all ...'

'Don't you worry. He'll come to a sticky end sooner or later. The chief problem, at present, is to raise this money for your journey. I suppose there isn't anybody you could borrow it from?'

But Arthur was already following another train of thought.

'I shall find a way out of this somehow.' His tone was considerably brighter. 'Just let me have time to think.'

While Arthur was thinking, a week went by. The weather

didn't improve. These dismal short days affected all our spirits. Frl. Schroeder complained of pains in the back. Arthur had a touch of liver. My pupils were unpunctual and stupid. I was depressed and cross. I began to hate our dingy flat, the shabby, staring house-front opposite my window, the damp street, the stuffy, noisy restaurant where we ate an economical supper, the burnt meat, the eternal sauerkraut, the soup.

'My God!' I exclaimed, one evening, to Arthur, 'what wouldn't I give to get out of this hole of a town for a day or two!'

Arthur, who had been picking his teeth in melancholy abstraction, looked at me thoughtfully. Rather to my surprise he seemed prepared to take a sympathetic interest in my grumbling.

'I must say, William, I'd noticed myself that you weren't in your accustomed sprightly vein. You're looking distinctly pale, you know.'

'Am I?'

'I fear you've been overworking yourself lately. You don't get out of doors enough. A young man like you needs exercise and fresh air.'

I smiled, amused and slightly mystified.

'You know, Arthur, you're getting quite the bedside manner.'

'My dear boy' – he pretended to be mildly hurt – 'I'm sorry that you mock my genuine concern for your health. After all, I'm old enough to be your father. I think I may be excused for sometimes feeling myself *in loco parentis*.'

'I beg your pardon, Daddy.'

Arthur smiled, but with a certain exasperation. I wasn't giving the right answers. He couldn't find an opening for the topic, whatever it was, which he was thus obscurely trying to broach. After a moment's hesitation, he tried again.

'Tell me, William, have you ever in the course of your travels, visited Switzerland?'

'For my sins. I once spent three months trying to learn French at a *pension* in Geneva.'

'Ah yes, I believe you told me.' Arthur coughed uneasily.

128

'But I was thinking more of the winter sports.'

'No. I've been spared those.'

Arthur appeared positively shocked.

'Really, my dear boy, if you don't mind my saying so, I think you carry your disdain of athleticism too far, I do indeed. Far be it for me to disparage the things of the mind. But, remember, you're still young. I hate to see you depriving yourself of pleasures which you won't, in any case, be able to indulge in later. Be quite frank; isn't it all rather a pose?'

I grinned.

'May I ask, with all due respect, what branch of sport you indulged in yourself at the age of twenty-eight?'

'Well – er – as you know, I have always suffered from delicate health. Our cases are not at all the same. Nevertheless, I may tell you that, during one of my visits to Scotland, I became quite an ardent fisherman. In fact, I frequently succeeded in catching those small fish with pretty red and brown markings. Their name escapes me for the moment.'

I laughed and lit a cigarette.

'And now, Arthur, having given such an admirable performance as the fond parent, suppose you tell me what you're driving at?'

He sighed, with resignation, with exasperation; partly, perhaps, with relief. He was excused from further shamming. When he spoke again, it was with a complete change of tone.

'After all, William, I don't know why I should beat about the bush. We've known each other long enough now. How long is it, by the way, since we first met?'

'More than two years.'

'Is it? Is it indeed? Let me see. Yes, you're right. As I was saying, we've known each other long enough now for me to be able to appreciate the fact that, although young in years, you're already a man of the world ...'

'You put it charmingly.'

'I assure you, I'm quite serious. Now, what I have to say is simply this (and please don't regard it as anything but the very vaguest possibility, because, quite apart from the question of your consent, a very vital question, I know, the whole thing would have to be approved by a third party, who doesn't, at present, know anything about the scheme) . . .'

Arthur paused, at the end of this parenthesis, to draw breath, and to overcome his constitutional dislike of laying his cards on the table.

'What I now merely ask you is this: would you, or would you not, be prepared to spend a few days in Switzerland this Christmas, at one or other of the winter sport resorts?'

Having got it out at last, he was covered in confusion, avoided my eye and began fiddling nervously with the cruet-stand. The neural effort required to make this offer appeared to have been considerable. I stared at him for a moment; then burst out laughing in my amazement.

'Well, I'm damned! So that *was* what you were after, all the time!'

Arthur joined, rather shyly, in my mirth. He was watching my face, shrewdly and covertly, in its various phases of astonishment. At what he evidently considered to be the psychological moment, he added:

'All expenses would be paid, of course.'

'But what on earth . . .' I began.

'Never mind, William. Never mind. It's just an idea of mine, that's all. It mayn't, it very likely won't, come to anything. Please don't ask me any more now. All I want to know is: would you be prepared to contemplate such a thing at all, or is it out of the question?'

'Nothing's out of the question, of course. But there are all sorts of things I should want to know. For instance . . .'

Arthur held up a delicate white hand.

'Not now, William, I beg.'

'Just this: What should I . . .'

'I can't discuss anything now,' interrupted Arthur, firmly. 'I simply must not.'

And, as if afraid that he would nevertheless be tempted to do so, he called to the waiter for our bills.

The best part of another week passed without Arthur having made any further allusion to the mysterious Swiss project. With considerable self-control, I refrained from reminding him of it; perhaps, like so many of his other brilliant schemes, it was already forgotten. And there were more important things to be thought of. Christmas was upon us, the year would soon be over; yet he hadn't so far as I knew, the ghost of a prospect of raising the money for his escape. When I asked him about it, he was vague. When I urged him to take steps, evasive. He seemed to be getting into a dangerous state of inertia. Evidently he underrated Schmidt's vindictiveness and power to harm. I did not. I couldn't so easily forget my last unpleasant glimpse of the secretary's face. Arthur's indifference drove me sometimes nearly frantic.

'Don't worry, dear boy,' he would murmur vaguely, with abstracted, butterfly fingerings of his superb wig. 'Sufficient unto the day, you know ... Yes.'

'A day will come,' I retorted, 'when it'll be sufficient unto two or three years' hard.'

Next morning, something happened to confirm my fears.

I was sitting in Arthur's room, assisting, as usual, at the ceremonies of the toilet, when the telephone bell rang.

'Will you be kind enough to see who it is, dear boy?' said Arthur, powder-puff in hand. He never personally answered a call if it could be avoided. I picked up the receiver.

'It's Schmidt,' I announced, a moment later, not without a certain gloomy satisfaction, covering the mouthpiece with my hand.

'Oh dear!' Arthur could hardly have been more flustered if his persecutor had actually been standing outside the bedroom door. Indeed, his harassed glance literally swept for an instant under the bed, as though measuring the available space for hiding there:

'Tell him anything. Say I'm not at home ...'

'I think,' I said firmly, 'that it'd be much better if you were to speak to him yourself. After all, he can't bite you. He may give you some idea of what he means to do.'

'Oh, very well, if you insist ...' Arthur was quite petulant. 'I must say, I should have thought it was very unnecessary.'

Gingerly, holding the powder-puff like a defensive weapon, he advanced to the instrument.

'Yes. Yes.' The dimple in his chin jerked sideways. He

snarled like a nervous lion. 'No ... no, really ... But do please listen one moment ... I can't, I assure you ... I can't ...'

His voice trailed off into a protesting, imploring whisper. He wobbled the hook of the receiver in futile distress.

'William, he's rung off.'

Arthur's dismay was so comic that I had to smile.

'What did he tell you?'

Arthur crossed the room and sat down heavily on the bed. He seemed quite exhausted. The powder-puff fell to the floor from between his limp fingers.

'I'm reminded of the dead adder, who heareth not the voice of the charmer ... What a monster, William! May your life never be burdened by such a fiend ...'

'Do tell me what he said?'

'He confined himself to threats, dear boy. Mostly incoherent. He wanted merely to remind me of his existence, I think. And that he'll need some more money soon. It was very cruel of you to make me speak to him. Now I shall be upset for the rest of the day. Just feel my hand; it's shaking like a leaf.'

'But, Arthur.' I picked up the powder-puff and put it on the dressing-table. 'It's no good just being upset. This must be a warning to you. You see, he really does mean business. We must do something about it. Haven't you any plan? Are there no steps you can take?'

Arthur roused himself with an effort.

'Yes, yes. You're right, of course. The die is cast. Steps shall be taken. In fact, not a moment shall be lost. I wonder if you'd be so good as to get me the *Fernamt* on the telephone and say I wish to put through a call to Paris? I don't think it's too early? No ...'

I asked for the number Arthur gave me and tactfully left him alone. I didn't see him again until the evening, when, as usual, we met by appointment at the restaurant for our supper. I noticed at once that he was brighter. He even insisted that we should drink wine, and when I demurred offered to pay my share of the bottle.

'It's so strengthening,' he added persuasively.

I grinned. 'Still worried about my health?'

'You're very unkind,' said Arthur, smiling. But he refused

to be drawn. When, a minute or two later, I asked point-blank how things were going, he replied:

'Let's have supper first, dear boy. Be patient with me, please.'

But even when supper was over and we had both ordered coffee (an additional extravagance), Arthur seemed in no hurry to give me his news. Instead, he appeared anxious to know what I had been doing, which pupils I had had, where I had lunched, and so forth.

'You haven't seen our friend Pregnitz lately, I think?'

'As a matter of fact, I'm going to tea with him tomorrow.'

'Are you, indeed?'

I restrained a smile. I was familiar enough by this time with Arthur's methods of approach. That new intonation in his voice, though suavely concealed, hadn't escaped me. So we were coming to the point at last.

'May I give him any message?'

Arthur's face was a comical study. We regarded each other with the amusement of two people who, night after night, cheat each other at a card game which is not played for money. Simultaneously we began to laugh.

'What, exactly,' I asked, 'do you want to get out of him?'

'William, please ... you put things so very crudely.'

'It saves time.'

'Yes, yes. You're right. Time is, alas, important just now. Very well, let's put it that I'm anxious to do a little business with him. Or shall we say to put him in the way of doing it for himself?'

'How very kind of you!'

Arthur tittered. 'I am kind, aren't I, William? That's what so few people seem to realize.'

'And what is this business? When is it coming off?'

'That remains to be seen. Soon, I hope.'

'I suppose you get a percentage?'

'Naturally.'

'A big percentage?'

'If it succeeds. Yes.'

'Enough for you to be able to leave Germany?'

'Oh, more than enough. Quite a nice little nest-egg, in fact.'

'Then that's splendid, isn't it?'

Arthur snarled nervously, regarded his finger-nails with extreme care.

'Unfortunately, there are certain technical difficulties. I need, as so often, your valuable advice.'

'Very well, let's hear them.'

Arthur considered for some moments. I could see that he was wondering how much he need tell me.

'Chiefly,' he said at length, 'that this business cannot be transacted in Germany.'

'Why not?'

'Because it would involve too much publicity. The other party to the deal is a well-known business man. As you probably know, big-business circles are comparatively small. They all watch each other. News gets round in a moment; the least hint is enough. If this man were to come to Berlin, the business people here would know about it before he'd even arrived. And secrecy is absolutely essential.'

'It all sounds very thrilling. But I'd no idea that Kuno was in business at all.'

'Strictly speaking, he isn't.' Arthur took some trouble to avoid my eye. 'This is merely a sideline.'

'I see. And where do you propose that this meeting shall take place?'

Arthur carefully selected a tooth-pick from the little bowl in front of him.

'That, my dear William, is where I hope to have the benefit of your valuable advice. It must be somewhere, of course, within easy reach of the German frontier. Somewhere where people can go, at this time of the year, without attracting attention, on a holiday.'

With great deliberation, Arthur broke the tooth-pick into two pieces and laid them side by side on the table-cloth. Without looking up at me, he added:

'Subject to your approval, I'd rather thought of Switzerland.'

There was quite a long pause. We were both smiling.

'So that's it?' I said at last.

Arthur redivided the tooth-pick into quarters; raised his

eyes to mine in a glance of dishonest, smiling innocence.

'That, as you rightly observe, dear boy, is it.'

'Well, well. What a foxy old thing you are.' I laughed. 'I'm beginning to see daylight at last.'

'I must confess, William, I was beginning to find you a little slow in the uptake. That isn't like you, you know.'

'I'm sorry, Arthur. But all these riddles make me a bit giddy. Suppose you stop asking them and let's have the whole yarn from the beginning?'

'I assure you, my dear boy, I'm more than ready to tell you all I know about this affair, which isn't very much. Well, to cut a long story short, Pregnitz is interested in one of the largest glass-works in Germany. It doesn't matter which. You wouldn't find his name on the list of directors; nevertheless, he has a great deal of unofficial influence. Of course, I don't pretend to understand these matters myself.'

'A glass-works? Well, that sounds harmless enough.'

'But, my dear boy,' Arthur was anxiously reassuring, 'of course it's harmless. You mustn't allow your naturally cautious nature to upset your sense of proportion. If this proposition sounds a little odd to you at first, it's only because you aren't accustomed to the ways of high finance. Why, it's the kind of thing which takes place every day. Ask anybody you like. The largest deals are almost always discussed informally.'

'All right! All right! Go on.'

'Let me see. Where was I? Ah, yes. Now, one of my most intimate friends in Paris is a certain prominent financier—'

'Who signs himself Margot?'

But this time I didn't catch Arthur off his guard. I couldn't even guess whether he was surprised or not. He merely smiled.

'How sharp you are, William! Well, perhaps he does. Anyhow, we'll call him Margot for convenience. Yes ... at all events, Margot is exceedingly anxious to have a chance of meeting Pregnitz. Although he doesn't admit it in so many words, I understand that he wishes to propose some sort of combine between Pregnitz's firm and his own. But that's entirely unofficial; it doesn't concern us. As for Pregnitz, he'll have to hear Margot's propositions for himself and decide whether they're to the advantage of his firm or not. Quite possibly, indeed probably, they will be. If not, there's no harm done. Margot will only have himself to blame. All he's asking me to arrange is that he meets the Baron socially, on neutral ground, where they won't be bothered by a lot of financial reporters and can talk things over quietly.'

'And as soon as you've brought them together, you get the cash?'

'When the meeting has taken place,' Arthur lowered his voice, 'I get half. The other half will be paid only if the deal is successful. But the worst of it is, Margot insists that he must see Pregnitz at once. He's always like that when once he gets an idea into his head. A most impatient man . . .'

'And he's really prepared to give you such a lot simply for arranging this meeting?'

'Remember, William, it seems a mere bagatelle to him. If this transaction is successful, he'll probably make millions.'

'Well, all I can say is, I congratulate you. It ought to be easy enough to earn.'

'I'm glad you think so, my dear boy.' Arthur's tone was guarded and doubtful.

'Why, where's the difficulty? All you have to do is to go to Kuno and explain the whole situation.'

'William!' Arthur seemed positively horror-stricken. 'That would be fatal!'

'I don't see why.'

'You don't see why? Really, dear boy, I must own I credited you with more finesse. No, that's entirely out of the question. You don't know Pregnitz as I do. He's extraordinarily sensitive in these matters, as I've discovered to my cost. He'd regard it as an unwarrantable intrusion into his affairs. He'd withdraw at once. He has the true aristocratic outlook, which one so seldom finds in these money-grubbing days. I admit I admire him for it.'

I grinned.

'He seems to be a very peculiar sort of business man, if he's offended when you offer him a fortune.'

But Arthur was quite heated.

'William, please, this is no time to be frivolous. Surely you must see my point. Pregnitz refuses, and I, for one, entirely agree with him, to mix personal with business relationships. Coming from you or from me, any suggestion that he should enter into negotiations with Margot, or with anybody else, would be an impertinence. And he'd resent it as such. Therefore, I do beg of you, don't breathe one word about this to him, on any account.'

'No, of course I won't. Don't get excited. But look here, Arthur, do I understand you to mean that Kuno is to go to Switzerland without knowing that he's there to meet Margot?'

'You put it in a nutshell.'

'H'm ... That certainly complicates things, rather. All the same, I don't see why you should have any special difficulty. Kuno probably goes to the winter sports, anyhow. It's quite in his line. What I don't altogether follow is, where do I come in? Am I to be brought along simply to swell the crowd, or to provide comic relief, or what?'

Arthur chose and divided another tooth-pick.

'I was just coming to that point, William.' His tone was carefully impersonal. 'I'm afraid, you see, you'd have to go alone.'

'Alone with Kuno?'

'Yes.' Arthur began speaking with nervous rapidity. 'There are a number of reasons which make it quite impossible for me to come with you, or to deal with this matter myself. In the first place, it would be exceedingly awkward, having once left this country, to return to it, as I should be obliged to do, even if only for a few days. Secondly, this suggestion, that we should go together to the winter sports, coming from me, would sound very odd. Pregnitz knows perfectly well that I haven't the constitution or the taste for such things. Coming from you, on the other hand, what could be more natural? He'd probably be only too delighted to travel with such a young and lively companion.'

'Yes, I quite see that ... but how should I get into touch with Margot? I don't even know him by sight.'

Arthur dismissed these difficulties with a wave of the hand.

'Leave that to me, dear boy, and to him. Set your mind at rest, forget everything I've told you this evening, and enjoy yourself.'

'Nothing but that?'

'Nothing. Once you've got Pregnitz across the frontier your duties are at an end.'

'It sounds delightful.'

Arthur's face lit up at once.

'Then you'll go?'

'I must think it over.'

Disappointed, he squeezed his chin. The tooth-picks were divided into eighths. At the end of a long minute, he said hesitantly:

'Quite apart from your expenses, which, as I think I told you, will be paid in advance, I should ask you to accept a little something, you know, for your trouble.'

'No, thank you, Arthur.'

'I beg your pardon, William.' He sounded much relieved. 'I might have known you wouldn't.'

I grinned.

'I won't deprive you of your honest earnings.'

Watching my face carefully, he smiled. He was uncertain how to take me. His manner changed.

'Of course, dear boy, you must do as you think best. I don't want to influence you in any way. If you decided against this scheme, I shan't allude to it again. At the same time, you know what it means to me. It's my only chance. I hate begging for favours. Perhaps I'm asking too much of you. I can only say that if you do this for me I shall be eternally grateful. And if it's ever in my power to repay you ...'

'Stop, Arthur. Stop! You'll make me cry.' I laughed. 'Very well. I'll do my best with Kuno. But, for Heaven's sake, don't build your hopes on it. I don't suppose for a minute he'll come. Probably he's engaged already.'

On this understanding, the subject was closed for the evening.

Next day, when I returned from the tea-party at Kuno's flat, I found Arthur waiting for me in his bedroom in a state
138

of the most extreme anxiety. He could hardly wait to shut the door before hearing my news.

'Quick, William, please. Tell me the worst. I can bear it. He won't come? No?'

'Yes,' I said. 'He'll come.'

For a moment, joy seemed to have made Arthur quite speechless, incapable of motion. Then a spasm passed over all his limbs, he executed a kind of caper in the air.

'My dear boy! I must, I really must embrace you!' And he literally threw his arms round my neck and kissed me, like a French general, on both cheeks. 'Tell me all about it. Did you have much difficulty? What did he say?'

'Oh, he more or less suggested the whole thing himself before I had opened my mouth. He wanted to go to the Riesengebirge, but I pointed out that the snow would be much better in the Alps.'

'You did? That was brilliant of you, William! Positively inspired ...'

I sat down in a chair. Arthur fluttered round me, admiring and delighted.

'You're quite sure he hasn't the least suspicion?'

'Perfectly sure.'

'And how soon shall you be able to start?'

'On Christmas Eve, I think.'

Arthur regarded me solicitously.

'You don't sound very enthusiastic, dear boy. I'd hoped this would be a pleasure to you, too. You're not feeling ill, by any chance, I trust?'

'Not in the least, thank you.' I stood up. 'Arthur, I'm going to ask you something.'

His eyelids fluttered nervously at my tone.

'Why – er – of course. Ask away, dear boy. Ask away.'

'I want you to speak the truth. Are you and Margot going to swindle Kuno? Yes or no?'

'My dear William – er – really ... I think you presume ...'

'I want an answer, please, Arthur. You see, it's important for me to know. I'm mixed up in this now. Are you or aren't you?'

'Well, I must say ... No. Of course not. As I've already explained at some length, I ...'

'Do you swear that?'

'Really, William, this isn't a court of law. Don't look at me like that, please. All right, if it gives you any satisfaction, I swear it.'

'Thank you. That's all I wanted. I'm sorry if I sounded rude. You know that, as a rule, I don't meddle in your affairs. Only this is my affair too, you see.'

Arthur smiled weakly, rather shaken.

'I quite understand your anxiety, dear boy, of course. But in this case, I do assure you, it's entirely unfounded. I've every reason to believe that Pregnitz will reap great benefits from this transaction, if he's wise enough to accept it.'

As a final test, I tried to look Arthur in the eyes. But no, this time-honoured process didn't work. Here were no windows to the soul. They were merely part of his face, light-blue jellies, like naked shell-fish in the crevices of a rock. There was nothing to hold the attention; no sparkle, no inward gleam. Try as I would, my glance wandered away to more interesting features; the soft, snout-like nose, the concertina chin. After three or four attempts, I gave it up. It was no good. There was nothing for it but to take Arthur at his word.

CHAPTER THIRTEEN

My journey with Kuno to Switzerland resembled the honey-moon trip which follows a marriage of convenience. We were polite, mutually considerate and rather shy. Kuno was a model of discreet attentiveness. With his own hands, he arranged my luggage in the rack, ran out at the last moment to buy me magazines, discovered by roundabout inquiries that I preferred the upper sleeping-car berth to the lower, and retired into the corridor to wait until I was undressed. When I got tired of reading, there he was, affable and informative, waiting to tell me the names of the mountains. We chatted with great animation in five-minute spasms, relapsing into sudden, abstracted silence. Both of us had plenty to think about. Kuno, I suppose, was worrying over the sinister manœuvres of German politics or dreaming about his island of the seven boys: I had leisure to review the Margot conun-drum in all its aspects. Did he really exist? Well, there above my head was a brand-new pigskin suitcase containing a dinner-jacket delivered from the tailor only the day before. Arthur had been positively lordly with our employer's money. 'Get whatever you want, dear boy. It would never do for you to be shabby. Besides, what a chance ...' After some hesita-tion, I had doubtfully followed his advice, though not to the reckless extent which he urged. Arthur even went so far in his interpretation of 'travelling expenses' as to press upon me a set of gold cuff-links, a wrist-watch, and a fountain-pen. 'After all, William, business is business. You don't know these people as I do.' His tone, when speaking of Margot, had become remarkably bitter: 'If you asked *him* to do any-thing for you he wouldn't hesitate to squeeze you to the last penny.'

On Boxing Day, our first morning, I awoke to the tinny jingle of sleigh-bells from the snowy street below, and a curious clicking noise, also metallic, which proceeded from the bathroom. Through the half-open door Kuno was to be seen, in a pair of gym shorts, doing exercises with a chest-expander. He was straining himself terribly; the veins in his neck bulged and his nostrils arched and stiffened with each desperate effort. He was obviously unaware that he was not alone. His eyes, bare of the monocle, were fixed in a short-sighted, visionary stare which suggested that he was engaged in a private religious rite. To speak to him would have been as intrusive as to disturb a man at his prayers. I turned over in bed and pretended to be asleep. After a few moments, I heard the bathroom door softly close.

Our rooms were on the first floor of the hotel, looking out over the houses of the village scattered along the frozen lake to the sparkling ski-ing slopes, massive and smooth as the contours of an immense body under blankets, crossed by the black spider-line of the funicular which climbed to the start of the toboggan runs. It seemed a curious background for an international business transaction. But, as Arthur had rightly said, I knew nothing of the ways of financiers. I got dressed slowly, thinking about my invisible host. Was Margot here already? The hotel was full up, the manager had told us. To judge from my glimpse of the guests, last night, in the huge dining-room, there must be several hundred of them staying here.

Kuno joined me for breakfast. He was dressed, with scrupulous informality, in grey flannel trousers, a blazer and the knotted silk scarf of his Oxford college colours.

'You slept well, I hope?'

'Very well, thank you. And you?'

'I, not so well.' He smiled, flushed, slightly abashed. 'It doesn't matter. In the night-time I had something to read, you see?'

Bashfully he let me see the title of the book he was holding in his hand. It was called *Billy the Castaway*.

'Is it good?' I asked.

'There is one chapter which is very nice, I find ...'

Before I could hear the contents of the nice chapter, however, a waiter appeared with our breakfast on a little wheeled car. We reverted at once to our self-conscious honeymoon manners.

'May I give you some cream?'

'Just a little, please.'

'Is this how you like it?'

'Thank you, that's delicious.'

Our voices sounded so absurd that I could have laughed out loud. We were like two unimportant characters in the first act of a play, put there to make conversation until it is time for the chief actor to appear.

By the time we had finished breakfast, the immense white slopes were infested already with tiny figures, some skimming and criss-crossing like dragon-flies, some faltering and collapsing like injured ants. The skaters were out in dozens on the lake. Within a roped enclosure, an inhumanly agile creature in black tights performed wonders before an attentive audience. Knapsacked, helmeted and booted, some of the more active guests were starting out on long, dangerous tours of the upper heights, like soldiers from a luxury barracks. And here and there, amidst the great army, the wounded were to be seen, limping on sticks or with their arms in slings, taking a painful convalescent promenade.

Attentive as ever, Kuno took it for granted that he was to teach me to ski. I should have much preferred to mess about alone, but my attempts at polite dissuasion were in vain. He regarded it as his duty; there was no more to be said. So we spent two perspiring hours on the beginners' slope; I slithering and stumbling, Kuno admonishing and supporting. 'No, excuse me, this is again not quite correct ... you hold yourself in too stiff a manner, you see?' His patience seemed inexhaustible. I longed for lunch.

About the middle of the morning, a young man came circling expertly among the novices in our neighbourhood. He stopped to watch us; perhaps my awkwardness amused him. His presence rather annoyed me; I didn't want an audience. Half by accident, half by design, I made a sudden swerve at him when he least expected it and knocked him clean off his feet. Our mutual apologies were profuse. He helped me to get up and even brushed some of the snow off me with his hand.

'Allow me ... van Hoorn.'

His bow, skis and all, was so marvellously stiff that he might have been challenging me to a duel.

'Bradshaw ... very pleased.'

I tried to parody it and promptly fell forward on my face, to be raised this time by Kuno himself. Somewhat less formally, I introduced them.

After this, to my relief, Kuno's interest in my instruction considerably decreased. Van Hoorn was a tall, fair boy, handsome in the severe Viking manner, though he had rather spoilt his appearance by shaving off most of his hair. The bald back of his head was sunburnt to an angry scarlet. He had studied for three semesters, he told us, at the University of Hamburg. He was furiously shy and blushed crimson whenever Kuno, with his discreetly flattering smile, addressed him.

Van Hoorn could do a turn which interested Kuno extremely. They went off for some distance to demonstrate and practise it. Presently, it was time for lunch. On our way down to the hotel, the young man introduced us to his uncle, a lively, plump little Dutchman, who was cutting figures on the ice with great skill. The elder Mr van Hoorn was a contrast to his grave nephew. His eyes twinkled merrily, he seemed delighted to make our acquaintance. His face was brown as an old boot and he was quite bald. He wore side-whiskers and a little pointed beard.

'So you've made some friends already?' He addressed his nephew in German. 'That's right.' His twinkling eyes regarded Kuno and myself. 'I tell Piet he should get to know a nice girl, but he won't; he's too shy. I wasn't like that at his age, I can tell you.'

Piet van Hoorn blushed, frowned and looked away, refusing to respond to Kuno's discreet glance of sympathy. Mr van Hoorn chattered away to me as he removed his skates.

'So you like it here? My word, so do I! I haven't enjoyed myself so much for years. I bet I've lost a pound or two already. Why, I don't feel a day over twenty-one, this morning.'

As we entered the dining-room, Kuno suggested that the van Hoorns should come and sit at our table; he gave a meaning glance at Piet as he spoke. I felt rather embarrassed. Kuno was certainly a bit crude in his advances. But Mr van Hoorn agreed at once, most heartily. He appeared to find nothing odd in the proposal. Probably he was glad enough to have some extra people to talk to.

During lunch, Kuno devoted himself almost entirely to Piet. He seemed to have succeeded in thawing the ice a little, for, several times, the boy laughed. Van Hoorn, meanwhile, was pouring into my ear a succession of the oldest and most childish smoking-room stories. He related them with extraordinary gusto and enjoyment. I scarcely listened. The warmth of the dining-room made me sleepy, after the sharp air outside; behind palms, the band played dreamy music. The food was delicious; seldom had I eaten such a lunch. And, all the time, I was vaguely wondering where Margot was, when and how he would appear.

Into my coma intruded, with increasing frequency, a few sentences of French. I could understand only a word here and there: 'interesting,' 'suggestive,' 'extremely typical.' It was the speaker's voice which caught my attention. It proceeded from the table next to our own. Idly I turned my head.

A large, middle-aged man sat facing an exotically pretty blonde girl of the type which Paris alone produces. Both of them were looking in our direction and speaking in carefully restrained tones, obviously about us. The man seemed particularly interested. He had a bald, egg-shaped head; bold, rudely prominent, round, solemn eyes; yellowish-white hair brushed back round the base of the skull like a pair of folded wings. His voice was vibrant and harsh. About his whole appearance there was something indescribably unpleasant and sinister. I felt a curious thrill pass through my nervous system; antagonistic, apprehensive, expectant. I glanced quickly at the others; but no, they seemed entirely unaware of the stranger's cynical, unconcealed inspection. Kuno was bending over to speak to Piet; fishy, caressing and suave. Mr van Hoorn had stopped talking at last and was making up for lost time on a grilled steak. He had tucked his napkin into his collar and

145

was chewing away with the abandonment of one who need no longer fear gravy-stains on his waistcoat. I fancied I heard our French neighbour pronounce the word '*dégoûtant.*'

I had frequently pictured to myself what Margot would look like. I had imagined him fatter, older, more prosaic. My imagination had been altogether too timid; I hadn't dreamed of anything so authentic, so absolutely, immediately convincing. Nobody's intuition could be at fault here. I was as certain of his identity as if I'd known him for years.

It was a thrilling moment. My only regret was that nobody could share its excitement with me. How Arthur would have enjoyed it! I could imagine his ill-concealed, gleeful agitation; his private signals which everybody would observe; his ludicrously forced attempts to cover up the mystery with bright chat. The very thought of them made me want to laugh out loud. I didn't dare risk another glance at our neighbours, lest they should see from my face what I knew. Long ago, I had made up my mind that never, at any stage in the proceedings, would I betray my complicity by so much as the flicker of an eyelid. Margot had kept his part of the bargain; I would show him that I, also, could be trustworthy and discreet.

How would he deliver his attack? This was a really fascinating question. I tried to put myself in his position; began to imagine the most extravagant subtleties. Perhaps he, or the girl, would pick Kuno's pocket and introduce themselves later, pretending to have found his note-case on the floor. Perhaps, that night, there would be a sham alarm of fire. Margot would plant smoke-bombs in Kuno's bedroom and then rush in to rescue him from the fumes. It seemed obvious to me that they would do something drastic. Margot didn't look the man to be content with half measures. What were they up to now? I could no longer hear their voices. Dropping my napkin somewhat clumsily on the floor, I bent down to pick it up and get a peep, only to find to my disappointment that the two of them had left the dining-room. I was disappointed, but, on thinking it over, not particularly surprised. This had been merely a reconnoitre. Margot would probably do nothing before the evening.

146

After lunch, Kuno earnestly advised me to rest. As a beginner, he explained, it would be most unwise for me to exert myself too much on the first day. I agreed, not without amusement. A few moments later, I heard him arranging with Piet van Hoorn to go out to the toboggan runs. Mr van Hoorn had already retired to his room.

At tea-time, there was dancing in the lounge. Piet and Kuno didn't appear; neither, to my relief, did Mr van Hoorn. I was quite happy by myself, watching the guests. Presently, Margot came in alone. He sat down on the opposite side of the big glass veranda, not more than a couple of yards from my table. Stealing a glance in his direction, I met his eyes. They were cold, prominent, rudely inquisitive as ever. My heart thumped uncomfortably. The situation was getting positively uncanny. Suppose I were to go over and speak to him now? I could save him, after all, a great deal of trouble. I had only to introduce him as an acquaintance of mine, met here by chance. There was no earthly reason why Kuno should suspect anything prearranged. Why should we go on performing this rather sinister charade? I hesitated, half rose to my feet, subsided again. For the second time my eyes met his. And now it seemed to me that I understood him perfectly. 'Don't be a little fool,' he was saying. 'Leave this to me. Don't try to meddle in things you don't understand.'

'All right,' I mentally told him, with a slight shrug of my shoulders. 'Do as you like. It's your funeral.'

And, feeling rather resentful, I got up and walked out of the lounge; I couldn't stand this silent *tête-à-tête* any longer.

At dinner, that night, both Kuno and Mr van Hoorn, in their different ways, were in high spirits. Piet looked bored. Perhaps he found his evening clothes as stiff and uncomfortable as I did mine. If so, he had my hearty sympathy. His uncle rallied him from time to time on his silence, and I reflected how much I should dislike to travel with Mr van Hoorn.

We were near the end of our meal when Margot and his companion came into the dining-room. I saw them at once, for I had been subconsciously keeping my eye on the door ever since we had sat down. Margot was wearing a tail-coat, with a flower in his button-hole. The girl was dressed magnificently, in some shimmering material which gleamed like silver armour. They passed down the long lane between the tables with many eyes following them.

'Look, Piet,' exclaimed Mr van Hoorn, 'there's a pretty girl for you. Ask her for a dance this evening. Her father won't bite you.'

To reach their table, Margot had to pass within a few inches of our chairs. As he did so, he briefly inclined his head. Kuno, ever gracious, returned the bow. For a moment, I thought Margot would follow up this opening, even if only with a conventional remark about the weather. He did not. The two of them took their places. Almost immediately, we rose to go and drink our coffee in the smoking-room.

Here, Mr van Hoorn's conversation took a surprising turn. It was as if he'd realized that the heartiness and the doubtful stories had been overdone. He began, quite suddenly, to talk about art. He had a house, he told us, in Paris, which was full of old furniture and etchings. Although he spoke modestly, it soon became clear that he was an expert. Kuno was greatly interested. Piet remained indifferent. I saw him cast more than one furtive glance at his wrist-watch, presumably to see whether it wasn't time for bed.

'Excuse me, gentlemen.'

The harsh voice startled all of us; nobody had seen Margot's approach. He towered above us, an elegant, sardonic figure, holding a cigar in his mottled, yellow hand.

'It is necessary that I ask this young man a question.'

His bulging eyes fixed upon Piet with a concentration which suggested that he was observing some minute insect, scarcely visible without the aid of a magnifying glass. The poor boy literally began to sweat with embarrassment. As for myself, I was so amazed at this new turn in Margot's tactics that I could only stare at him, my mouth hanging open. Margot himself evidently enjoyed the effect which his dramatic appearance had created. His lips curved in a smile which was positively diabolic.

'Have you the true Aryan descent?'

And before the astounded Piet could answer, he added:

148

'I am Marcel Janin.'

I don't know whether the others had really heard of him, or whether their polite interest was merely pretended. As it happened, I knew his name quite well. M. Janin was one of Fritz Wendel's favourite authors. Fritz had once lent me a book of his – *The Kiss Under the Midnight Sun*. It was written in the fashionable French manner, half romance, half reportage, and gave a lurid, obviously imaginative account of the erotic life of Hammerfest. And there were half a dozen others, equally sensational and ranging in *milieu* from Santiago to Shanghai. M. Janin's particular brand of pornography, if one was to judge from his clothes, appeared to have hit the public taste. He had just finished his eighth, he told us: it dealt with the amours peculiar to a winter sport hotel. Hence his presence here. After his brusque self-introduction, he proved most affable and treated us, without further request, to a discourse on his career, aims and methods of work.

'I write very quick,' he informed us. 'For me, one glance is sufficient. I do not believe in the second impression.'

A couple of days ashore from a cruising liner had furnished M. Janin with the material for most of his works. And now Switzerland was disposed of, too. Looking for fresh worlds to conquer, he had fixed on the Nazi movement. He and his secretary were leaving next day for Munich. 'Within a week,' he concluded ominously, 'I shall know all.'

I wondered what part M. Janin's secretary (he insisted, several times, on this title), played in his lightning researches. Probably she acted as a kind of rough and ready chemical reagent; in certain combinations she produced certain known results. It was she, it seemed, who had discovered Piet. M. Janin, as excited as a hunter in unfamiliar territory, had rushed, over-precipitately, to the attack. He didn't seem much disappointed, however, to discover that this wasn't his legitimate prey. His generalizations, formulated, to save time, in advance, were not easily disturbed. Dutchman or German, it was all grist to the mill. Piet, I suspected, would nevertheless make his appearance in the new book, dressed up in a borrowed brown shirt. A writer with M. Janin's technique can afford to waste nothing.

One mystery was solved, the other deepened. I puzzled over it for the rest of the evening. If Margot wasn't Janin, who was he? And where? It seemed odd that he should fritter away twenty-four hours like this, after being in such a hurry to get Kuno to come. Tomorrow, I thought, he'll turn up for certain. My meditations were interrupted by Kuno tapping at my door to ask if I had gone to bed. He wanted to talk about Piet van Hoorn, and, sleepy as I felt, I wasn't unkind enough to deny him.

'Tell me, please . . . don't you find him a little like Tony?'

'Tony?' I was stupid this evening. 'Tony who?'

Kuno regarded me with gentle reproach.

'Why, excuse me . . . I mean Tony in the book, you see.'

I smiled.

'You think Tony is more like Piet than like Heinz?'

'Oh yes,' Kuno was very definite on this point. 'Much more like.'

So poor Heinz was banished from the island. Having reluctantly agreed to this, we said good-night.

Next morning I decided to make some investigations for myself. While Kuno was in the lounge talking to the van Hoorns, I got into conversation with the hall porter. Oh yes, he assured me, a great many business people were here from Paris just now; some of them very important.

'M. Bernstein, for instance, the factory-owner. He's worth millions . . . Look, sir, he's over there now, by the desk.'

I had just time to catch sight of a fat, dark man with an expression on his face like that of a sulky baby. I had never noticed him anywhere in our neighbourhood. He passed through the doors into the smoking-room, a bundle of letters in his hand.

'Do you know if he owns a glass factory?' I asked.

'I'm sure I couldn't say, sir. I wouldn't be surprised. They say he's got his finger in nearly everything.'

The day passed without further developments. In the afternoon, Mr van Hoorn at length succeeded in forcing his bashful nephew into the company of some lively Polish girls. They all went off ski-ing together. Kuno was not best pleased, but he accepted the situation with his usual grace. He seemed to have developed quite a taste for Mr van Hoorn's society. The two of them spent the afternoon indoors.

After tea, as we were leaving the lounge, we came face to face with M. Bernstein. He passed us by without the faintest interest.

As I lay in bed that night I almost reached the conclusion that Margot must be a figment of Arthur's imagination. For what purpose he had been created I couldn't conceive. Nor did I much care. It was very nice here. I was enjoying myself; in a day or two I should have learnt to ski. I would make the most of my holiday, I decided; and, following Arthur's advice, forget the reasons for which I had come. As for Kuno, my fears had been unfounded. He hadn't been cheated out of a farthing. So what was there to worry about?

On the afternoon of the third day of our visit, Piet suggested, of his own accord, that we two should go skating on the lake alone. The poor boy, as I had noticed at lunch, was near bursting-point. He had had more than enough of his uncle, of Kuno and of the Polish girls; it had become necessary for him to vent his feelings on somebody, and, of a bad bunch, I seemed the least unlikely to be sympathetic. No sooner were we on the ice than he started: I was astonished to find how much and with what vehemence he could talk.

What did I think of this place? he asked. Wasn't all this luxury sickening? And the people? Weren't they too idiotic and revolting for words? How could they behave as they did, with Europe in its present state? Had they no decency at all? Had they no national pride, to mix with a lot of Jews who were ruining their countries? How did I feel about it, myself?

'What does your uncle say to it all?' I counter-questioned, to avoid an answer.

Piet shrugged his shoulders angrily.

'Oh, my uncle ... he doesn't take the least interest in politics. He only cares for his old pictures. He's more of a Frenchman than a Dutchman, my father says.'

Piet's studies in Germany had turned him into an ardent

Fascist. M. Janin's instinct hadn't been so incorrect, after all. The young man was browner than the Browns.

'What my country needs is a man like Hitler. A real leader. A people without ambition is unworthy to exist.' He turned his handsome, humourless face and regarded me sternly. 'You, with your Empire, you must understand that.'

But I refused to be drawn.

'Do you often travel with your uncle?' I asked.

'No. As a matter of fact I was surprised when he asked me to come with him here. At such short notice, too; only a week ago. But I love ski-ing, and I thought it would all be quite primitive and simple, like the tour I made with some students last Christmas. We went to the Riesengebirge. We used to wash ourselves every morning with snow in a bucket. One must learn to harden the body. Self-discipline is most important in these times . . .'

'Which day did you arrive here?' I interrupted.

'Let's see. It must have been the day before you did.' A thought suddenly struck Piet. He became more human. He even smiled. 'By the way, that's a funny thing I'd quite forgotten . . . my uncle was awfully keen to get to know you.'

'To know me?'

'Yes . . .' Piet laughed and blushed. 'As a matter of fact, he told me to try and find out who you were.'

'He did?'

'You see, he thought you were the son of a friend of his; an Englishman. But he'd only met the son once, a long time ago, and he wasn't sure. He was afraid that, if you saw him and he didn't recognize you, you'd be offended.'

'Well, I certainly helped you to make my acquaintance, didn't I?'

We both laughed.

'Yes, you did.'

'Ha ha! How very funny.'

'Yes, isn't it? Very funny indeed.'

When we returned to the hotel for tea, we had some trouble in finding Kuno and Mr van Hoorn. They were sitting together in a remote corner of the smoking-room, at a distance from the other guests. Mr van Hoorn was no longer laughing; he spoke quietly and seriously, with his eyes on Kuno's face. And Kuno himself was as grave as a judge. I had the impression that he was profoundly disturbed and perplexed by the subject of their conversation. But this was only an impression, and a momentary one. As soon as Mr van Hoorn became aware of my approach, he laughed loudly and gave Kuno's elbow a nudge, as if reaching the climax of a funny story. Kuno laughed too, but with less enthusiasm.

'Well, well!' exclaimed Mr van Hoorn. 'Here are the boys! As hungry as hunters, I'll be bound! And we two old fogies have been wasting the whole afternoon yarning away indoors. My goodness, is it as late as that? I say, I want my tea!'

'A telegram for you, sir,' said the voice of a page-boy, just behind me. I stepped aside, supposing that he was addressing one of the others, but no; he held the silver tray towards me. There was no mistake. On the envelope, I read my name.

'Aha!' cried Mr van Hoorn. 'Your sweetheart's getting impatient. She wants you to go back to her.'

I tore open the envelope, unfolded the paper. The message was only three words:

Please return immediately.

I read it over several times. I smiled.

'As a matter of fact,' I told Mr van Hoorn, 'you're quite right. She does.'

The telegram was signed 'Ludwig.'

Something had happened to Arthur. That much was obvious. Otherwise, if he'd wanted me, he'd have sent for me himself. And the mess he was in, whatever it was, must have something to do with the Party, since Bayer had signed the telegram. Here my reasoning came to an end. It was bounded by guesses and possibilities as vague and limitless as the darkness which enclosed the train. Lying in my berth, I tried to sleep and couldn't. The swaying of the coach, the clank of the wheels kept time with the excited, anxious throbbing of my heart. Arthur, Bayer, Margot, Schmidt; I tried to puzzle backwards, sideways, all ways up. It kept me awake the whole night.

Years later, it seemed, though, actually, only the next afternoon, I let myself into the flat with the latch-key; quietly pushed open the door of my room. In the middle of it sat Frl. Schroeder, dozing, in the best arm-chair. She had taken off her slippers and was resting her stockinged feet on the footstool. When one of her lodgers was away, she often did this. She was indulging in the dream of most landladies, that the whole place was hers.

If I had returned from the dead, she could hardly have uttered a more piercing scream on waking and seeing my figure in the doorway.

'Herr Bradshaw! How you startled me!'

'I'm sorry, Frl. Schroeder. No, please don't get up. Where's Herr Norris?'

'Herr Norris?' She was still a bit dazed. 'I don't know, I'm sure. He said he'd be back about seven.'

'He's still living here, then?'

'Why, of course, Herr Bradshaw. What an idea!' Frl. Schroeder regarded me with astonishment and anxiety. 'Is anything the matter? Why didn't you let me know that you were coming home sooner? I was going to have given your room a thorough turn-out tomorrow.'

'That's perfectly all right. I'm sure everything looks very nice. Herr Norris hasn't been ill, has he?'

'Why, no.' Frl. Schroeder's perplexity was increasing with every moment. 'That is, if he has he hasn't said a word about it to me, and he's been up and about from morning to midnight. Did he write and tell you so?'

'Oh no, he didn't do that ... only ... when I went away I thought he looked rather pale. Has anybody rung for me or left any messages?'

'Nothing, Herr Bradshaw. You remember, you told all your pupils you would be away until the New Year.'

'Yes, of course.'

I walked over to the window, looked down into the dank, empty street. No, it wasn't quite empty. Down there, on the corner, stood a small man in a buttoned-up overcoat and a felt hat. He paced quietly up and down, his hands folded behind his back, as if waiting for a girl friend.

'Shall I get you some hot water?' asked Frl. Schroeder tactfully. I caught sight of myself in the mirror. I looked tired, dirty and unshaved.

'No, thank you,' I said, smiling. 'There's something I've got to attend to first. I shall be back in about an hour. Perhaps you'd be so kind and heat the bath?'

'Yes, Ludwig's here,' the girls in the outer office at the Wilhelmstrasse told me. 'Go right in.'

Bayer didn't seem in the least surprised to see me. He looked up from his papers with a smile.

'So here you are, Mr Bradshaw! Please sit down. You have enjoyed your holiday, I hope?'

I smiled.

'Well, I was just beginning to ...'

'When you got my telegram? I am sorry, but it was necessary, you see.'

Bayer paused; regarded me thoughtfully; continued:

'I'm afraid that what I have to say may be unpleasant for you, Mr Bradshaw. But it is not right that you are kept any longer in ignorance of the truth.'

I could hear a clock ticking somewhere in the room;

everything seemed to have become very quiet. My heart was thumping uncomfortably against my ribs. I suppose that I half guessed what was coming.

'You went to Switzerland,' Bayer continued, 'with a certain Baron Pregnitz?'

'Yes. That's right.' I licked my lips with my tongue.

'Now I am going to ask you a question which may seem that I interfere very much in your private affairs. Please do not be offended. If you do not wish it, you will not answer, you understand?'

My throat had gone dry. I tried to clear it, and made an absurdly loud, grating sound.

'I'll answer any question you like,' I said, rather huskily.

Bayer's eyes brightened approvingly. He leant forward towards me across the writing-table.

'I am glad that you take this attitude, Mr Bradshaw ... You wish to help us. That is good ... Now, will you tell me, please, what was the reason which Norris gave you that you should go with this Baron Pregnitz to Switzerland?'

Again I heard that clock. Bayer, his elbows resting on the table, regarded me benevolently, with encouraging attention. For the second time, I cleared my throat.

'Well,' I began, 'first of all, you see ...'

It was a long silly story, which seemed to take hours to tell. I hadn't realized how foolish, how contemptible some of it would sound. I felt horribly ashamed of myself, blushed, tried to be humorous and weakly failed, defended and then accused my motives, avoided certain passages, only to blurt them out a moment later, under the neutral inquisition of his friendly eyes. The story seemed to involve a confession of all my weaknesses to that silent, attentive man. I have never felt so humiliated in my life.

When, at last, I had finished, Bayer made a slight movement.

'Thank you, Mr Bradshaw. All this, you see, is very much as we had supposed ... Our workers in Paris know this Mr van Hoorn already very well. He is a clever man. He has given us much trouble.'

'You mean ... that he's a police agent?'

'Unofficially, yes. He collects information of all kinds and sells it to those who will pay him. There are many who do this; but most of them are quite stupid and not dangerous at all.'

'I see ... And van Hoorn's been making use of Norris to collect information?'

'That is so. Yes.'

'But how on earth did he get Norris to help him? What story did he tell him? I wonder Norris wasn't suspicious.'

In spite of his gravity, Bayer's eyes showed a sparkle of amusement.

'It is possible that Norris was most suspicious indeed. No. You have misunderstood me, Mr Bradshaw. I have not said that van Hoorn deceived him. That was not necessary.'

'Not necessary?' I stupidly echoed.

'Not necessary. No ... Norris was quite aware, you see, of what van Hoorn wanted. They understood each other very well. Since Norris returned to Germany, he has been receiving regularly sums of money through van Hoorn from the French Secret Service.'

'I don't believe it!'

'Nevertheless, it is true. I can prove it, if you wish. Norris has been paid to keep an eye on us, to give information about our plans and movements.' Bayer smiled and raised his hand, as if to anticipate a protest. 'Oh, this is not so terrible as it sounds. The information which he had to give was of no importance. In our movement, we have not the necessity to make great plots, as are described of us in the capitalist Press and the criminal romances. We act openly. It is easy for all to know what we do. It is possible that Norris can have been able to tell his friends the names of some of our messengers who are going frequently between Berlin and Paris. And, perhaps, also, certain addresses. But this can have been only at the first.'

'You've known about him a long time already, then?' I hardly recognized the sound of my own voice.

Bayer smiled brilliantly.

'Quite a long time. Yes.' His tone was soothing. 'Norris has even been very helpful to us, though he did not wish it.

We were able, occasionally, to convey much false impressions to our opponents through this channel.'

With bewildering speed, the jig-saw puzzle was fitting itself together in my brain. In a flash, another piece was added. I remembered the morning after the elections; Bayer in this very room, handing Arthur the sealed packet from his writing-table drawer.

'Yes ... I see now ...'

'My dear Mr Bradshaw,' Bayer's tone was kind, almost paternal, 'please do not distress yourself too much. Norris is your friend, I know. Mind, I have not said this against him as a man; the private life is not our concern. We are all convinced that you cannot have known of this. You have acted throughout with good faith towards us. I wish it had been possible to keep you in ignorance over this matter.'

'What I still don't understand is, how Pregnitz ...'

'Ah, I am coming to that ... Norris, you see, found himself unable any longer to satisfy his Paris friends with these reports. They were so often insufficient or false. And so he proposed to van Hoorn the idea of a meeting with Pregnitz.'

'And the glass factory?'

'It exists only in the imagination of Norris. Here he made use of your inexperience. It was not for this that van Hoorn paid your expenses to Switzerland. Baron Pregnitz is a politician, not a financier.'

'You don't mean ...?'

'Yes, this is what I wished to tell you. Pregnitz has access to many secrets of the German Government. It is possible for him to obtain copies of maps, plans and private documents which van Hoorn's employers will pay very much to see. Perhaps Pregnitz will be tempted. This does not concern us. We wish only to warn you personally, that you may not discover yourself innocently in a prison for the high treason.'

'My God ... how on earth did you get to know all this?'

Bayer smiled.

'You think that we have also our spies? No, that is not necessary. All information of this sort one can obtain so easily from the police.'

'Then the police know?'

'I do not think that they know all for certain, yet. But they are very suspicious. Two of them came here to ask us questions concerning Norris, Pregnitz and yourself. From these questions one could guess a good deal. I believe we have satisfied them that you are not a dangerous conspirator,' Bayer smiled, 'nevertheless, it seemed best to telegraph to you at once, that you might not be further involved.'

'It was very good of you to bother what became of me at all.'

'We try always to help those who help us; although, unfortunately, this is sometimes not possible. You have not seen Norris yet?'

'No. He was out when I arrived.'

'So? That is excellent. It is better that you should tell him these things yourself. Since a week he has not been here. Tell him, please, that we wish him no harm; but it will be better for himself if he goes away from Germany at once. And warn him, also, that the police have him under observance. They are opening all letters which he receives or writes; of this I am sure.'

'All right,' I said, 'I'll tell him that.'

'You will? That is good.' Bayer rose to his feet. 'And now, Mr Bradshaw, please do not make yourself reproaches. You have been foolish, perhaps. Never mind; we are all sometimes very, very foolish. You have done nothing to be ashamed. I think that now you will be more careful with whom you make a friend, eh?'

'Yes, I shall.'

Bayer smiled. He clapped me encouragingly on the shoulder.

'Then now we will forget this unpleasant matter. You would like to do some more work for us soon? Excellent ... You tell Norris what I said, eh? Good-bye.'

'Good-bye.'

I shook hands with him, I suppose, and got myself off the premises in the usual manner. I must have behaved quite normally, because nobody in the outer office stared. It was only when I was out in the street that I began to run.

I was suddenly in a tremendous hurry; I wanted to get this over, quick.

A taxi passed; I was inside it before the driver had had time to slow down. 'Drive as fast as you can,' I told him. We skidded in and out of the traffic; it had been raining and the roadway was slimy with mud. The lamps were lighted already; it was getting dark. I lit a cigarette and threw it away after a couple of puffs. My hands were trembling, otherwise I was perfectly calm, not angry, not even disgusted; nothing. The puzzle fitted together perfectly. I could see it all, if I wished to look at it, a compact, vivid picture, at a single glance. All I want, I thought, is to get this over. Now.

Arthur was back already. He looked out of his bedroom as I opened the front door of the flat.

'Come in, dear boy! Come in! This is indeed a pleasant surprise! When Frl. Schroeder told me you'd returned, I could hardly believe it. What was it made you come back so soon? Were you homesick for Berlin; or did you pine for my society? Please say you did! We've all missed you very much here. Our Christmas dinner was tasteless indeed without you. Yes ... I must say, you're not looking as well as I'd expected; perhaps you're tired after the journey? Sit down here. Have you had tea? Let me give you a glass of something to refresh you?'

'No, thank you, Arthur.'

'You won't? Well, well ... perhaps you'll change your mind later. How did you leave our friend Pregnitz? Flourishing, I hope?'

'Yes. He's all right.'

'I'm glad to hear that. Very glad. And now, William, I really must congratulate you on the admirable skill and tact with which you fulfilled your little mission. Margot was more than satisfied. And he's very particular, you know; very difficult to please ...'

'You've heard from him, then?'

'Oh, yes. I got a long telegram this morning. The money will arrive tomorrow. I'm bound to say this for Margot: he's most punctual and correct in these matters. One can always rely on him.'

'Do you mean to say that Kuno's agreed?'

'No, not that, alas. Not yet. These things aren't settled in a day. But Margot's distinctly hopeful. It seems that Pregnitz was a little difficult to persuade at first. He didn't quite see how this transaction would be of advantage to his firm. But now he's become definitely interested. He wants time to think it over, of course. Meanwhile, I get half my share as we arranged. I'm thankful to say that it's more than sufficient to cover my travelling expenses; so that's one weight lifted from my mind. As for the rest, I'm convinced, personally, that Pregnitz will agree in the end.'

'Yes ... I suppose they all do.'

'Nearly all, yes ...' Arthur agreed absently; became aware, the next moment, of something strange in my tone. 'I don't think, William, I quite understand what you mean.'

'Don't you? I'll put it more plainly then: I suppose van Hoorn usually succeeds in getting people to sell him whatever he wants to buy?'

'Well, er – I don't know that, in this case, one could describe it as a sale. As I think I told you ...'

'Arthur,' I interrupted wearily, 'you can stop lying now. I know all about it.'

'Oh,' he began, and was silent. The shock seemed to have taken away his breath. Sinking heavily into a chair, he regarded his finger-nails with unconcealed dismay.

'This is all my own fault, really, I suppose. I was a fool ever to have trusted you. To do you justice, you more or less warned me against it, often enough.'

Arthur looked up at me quickly, like a spaniel which is going to be whipped. His lips moved, but he didn't speak. The deep-cleft dimple appeared for a moment in his collapsed chin. Furtively, he scratched his jowl, withdrawing his hand again immediately, as though he were afraid this gesture might annoy me.

'I ought to have known that you'd find a use for me, sooner or later; even if it was only as a decoy duck. You always find a use for everybody, don't you? If I'd landed up in prison it'd have damn' well served me right.'

'William, I give you my word of honour, I never ...'

'I won't pretend,' I continued, 'that I care a damn what happens to Kuno. If he's fool enough to let himself in for this, he does it with his eyes open ... But I must say this, Arthur: if anybody but Bayer had told me you'd ever do the dirty on the Party, I'd have called him a bloody liar. You think that's very sentimental of me, I suppose?'

Arthur started visibly at the name.

'So Bayer knows, does he?'

'Of course.'

'Oh dear, oh dear ...'

He seemed to have collapsed into himself, like a scarecrow in the rain. His loose, stubbly cheeks were blotched and pallid, his lips parted in a vacant snarl of misery.

'I never really told van Hoorn anything of importance, William. I swear to you I didn't.'

'I know. You never got the chance. It doesn't seem to me that you're much good, even as a crook.'

'Don't be angry with me, dear boy. I can't bear it.'

'I'm not angry with you; I'm angry with myself for being such an idiot. I thought you were my friend, you see.'

'I don't ask you to forgive me,' said Arthur, humbly. 'You'll never do that, of course. But don't judge me too harshly. You're young. Your standards are so severe. When you get to my age, you'll see things differently, perhaps. It's very easy to condemn when one isn't tempted. Remember that.'

'I don't condemn you. As for my standards, if I ever had any, you've muddled them up completely. I expect you're right. In your place, I'd probably have done just the same.'

'You see?' Arthur eagerly followed up his advantage. 'I knew you'd come to look at it in that light.'

'I don't want to look at it in any light. I'm too utterly sick of the whole filthy business ... My God, I wish you'd go away somewhere where I'll never see you again!'

Arthur sighed.

'How hard you are, William. I should never have expected

it. You always seemed to me to have such a sympathetic nature.'

'That was what you counted on, I suppose? Well, I think you'll find that the soft ones object to being cheated even more than the others. They mind it more because they feel that they've only themselves to blame.'

'You're perfectly justified, of course. I deserve all the unkind things you say. Don't spare me. But I promise you most solemnly, the thought that I was implicating you in any sort of crime never once entered my head. You see, everything has gone off exactly as we planned. After all, where was the risk?'

'There was more risk than you think. The police knew all about our little expedition before we'd even started.'

'The police? William, you're not in earnest!'

'You don't think I'm trying to be funny, do you? Bayer told me to warn you. They've been round to see him and make inquiries.'

'My God ...'

The last traces of stiffness had gone out of Arthur. He sat there like a crumpled paper bag, his blue eyes vivid with terror.

'But they can't possibly ...'

I went to the window.

'Come and look, if you don't believe me. He's still there.'

'Who's still there?'

'The detective who's watching this house.'

Without a word, Arthur hurried to my side at the window and took a peep at the man in the buttoned-up overcoat.

Then he went slowly back to his chair. He seemed suddenly to have become much calmer.

'What am I to do?' He appeared to be thinking aloud rather than addressing me.

'You must clear out, of course; the moment you've got this money.'

'They'll arrest me, William.'

'Oh no, they won't. They'd have done it before this, if they were going to. Bayer says they've been reading all your letters ... Besides, they don't know everything for certain yet, he thinks.'

Arthur pondered for some minutes in silence. He looked up at me in nervous appeal.

'Then you're not going to ...' He stopped.

'Not going to what?'

'To tell them, well – er – everything?'

'My God, Arthur!' I literally gasped. 'What, exactly, do you take me for?'

'No, of course, dear boy ... Forgive me. I might have known ...' Arthur coughed apologetically. 'Only, just for the moment, I was afraid. There might be quite a large reward, you see ...'

For several seconds I was absolutely speechless. Seldom have I been so shocked. Open-mouthed, I regarded him with a mixture of indignation and amusement, curiosity and disgust. Timidly, his eyes met mine. There could be no doubt about it. He was honestly unaware of having said anything to surprise or offend. I found my voice at last.

'Well, of all the ...'

But my outburst was cut short by a furious volley of knocks on the bedroom door.

'Herr Bradshaw! Herr Bradshaw!' Frl. Schroeder was in frantic agitation. 'The water's boiling and I can't turn on the tap! Come quick this moment, or we shall all be blown to bits!'

'We'll discuss this later,' I told Arthur, and hurried out of the room.

CHAPTER FIFTEEN

Three-quarters of an hour later, washed and shaved, I returned to Arthur's room. I found him peering cautiously down into the street from behind the shelter of the lace curtain.

'There's a different one there now, William,' he told me. 'They relieved each other about five minutes ago.'

His tone was gleeful; he seemed positively to be enjoying the situation. I joined him at the window. Sure enough, a tall man in a bowler hat had taken the place of his colleague at the thankless task of waiting for the invisible girl friend.

'Poor fellow,' Arthur giggled, 'he looks terribly cold, doesn't he? Do you think he'd be offended if I sent him down a medicine bottle full of brandy, with my card?'

'He mightn't see the joke.'

Strangely enough, it was I who felt embarrassed. With indecent ease, Arthur seemed to have forgotten all the unpleasant things I had said to him less than an hour before. His manner towards me was as natural as if nothing had happened. I felt myself harden towards him again. In my bath, I had softened, regretted some cruel words, condemned others as spiteful or priggish. I had rehearsed a partial reconciliation, on magnanimous terms. But Arthur, of course, was to make the advances. Instead of which, here he was, blandly opening his wine-cupboard with his wonted hospitable air.

'At any rate, William, you won't refuse a glass yourself? It'll give you an appetite for supper.'

'No, thank you.'

I tried to make my tone stern; it sounded merely sulky. Arthur's face fell at once. His ease of manner, I saw now, had been only experimental. He sighed deeply, resigned to further penitence, assuming an expression which was like a funeral top-hat, lugubrious, hypocritical, discreet. It became him so ill, that in spite of myself, I had to smile.

'It's no good, Arthur. I can't keep it up!'

He was too cautious to reply to this, except with a shy, sly smile. This time, he wasn't going to risk an over-hasty response.

'I suppose,' I continued reflectively, 'that none of them were ever really angry with you, were they, afterwards?'

Arthur didn't pretend to misunderstand. Demurely he inspected his finger-nails.

'Not everybody, alas, has your generous nature, William.'

It was no good; we had returned to our verbal card-playing. The moment of frankness, which might have redeemed so much, had been elegantly avoided. Arthur's orientally sensitive spirit shrank from the rough, healthy, modern catch-as-catch-can of home-truths and confessions; he offered me a compliment instead. Here we were, as so often before, at the edge of that delicate, almost invisible line which divided our two worlds. We should never cross it now. I wasn't old or subtle enough to find the approach. There was a disappointing pause, during which he rummaged in the cupboard.

'Are you *quite* sure you won't have a drop of brandy?'

I sighed. I gave him up. I smiled.

'All right. Thanks. I will.'

We drank ceremoniously, touching glasses. Arthur smacked his lips with unconcealed satisfaction. He appeared to imagine that something had been symbolized: a reconciliation, or, at any rate, a truce. But no, I couldn't feel this. The ugly, dirty fact was still there, right under our noses, and no amount of brandy could wash it away.

Arthur appeared, for the moment, sublimely unconscious of its existence. I was glad. I felt a sudden anxiety to protect him from a realization of what he had done. Remorse is not for the elderly. When it comes to them, it is not purging or uplifting, but merely degrading and wretched, like a bladder disease. Arthur must never repent. And indeed, it didn't seem probable that he ever would.

'Let's go out and eat,' I said, feeling that the sooner we got out of this ill-omened room the better. Arthur cast an involuntary glance in the direction of the window.

'Don't you think, William, that Frl. Schroeder would make us some scrambled eggs? I hardly feel like venturing out of doors, just now.'

'Of course we must go out, Arthur. Don't be silly. You must behave as normally as possible, or they'll think you're hatching some plot. Besides, think of that unfortunate man down there. How dull it must be for him. Perhaps, if we go out, he'll be able to get something to eat, too.'

'Well, I must confess,' Arthur doubtfully agreed. 'I hadn't thought of it in that light. Very well, if you're quite sure it's wise ...'

It is a curious sensation to know that you are being followed by a detective; especially when, as in this case, you are actually anxious not to escape him. Emerging into the street, at Arthur's side, I felt like the Home Secretary leaving the House of Commons with the Prime Minister. The man in the bowler hat was either a novice at his job or exceedingly bored with it. He made no attempt at conceal-ment; stood staring at us from the middle of a pool of lamplight. A sort of perverted sense of courtesy prevented me from looking over my shoulder to see if he was following; as for Arthur, his embarrassment was only too painfully visible. His neck seemed to telescope into his body, so that three-quarters of his face was hidden by his coat collar; his gait was that of a murderer retreating from a corpse. I soon noticed that I was subconsciously regulating my pace; I kept hurrying forward in an instinctive desire to get away from our pursuer, then slowing down, lest we should leave him altogether behind. During the walk to the restaurant, Arthur and I didn't exchange a word.

Barely had we taken our seats when the detective entered. Without a glance in our direction, he strode over to the bar and was soon morosely consuming a boiled sausage and a glass of lemonade.

'I suppose,' I said, 'that they're not allowed to drink beer when they're on duty.'

'Ssh, William!' giggled Arthur, 'he'll hear you!'

'I don't care if he does. He can't arrest me for laughing at him.'

Nevertheless, such is the latent power of one's upbringing, I lowered my voice almost to a whisper.

'I suppose they pay him his expenses. You know, we really ought to have taken him to the Montmartre and given him a treat.'

'Or to the opera.'

'It'd be rather amusing to go to church.'

We sniggered together, like two boys poking fun at the schoolmaster. The tall man, if he was aware of our comments, bore himself with considerable dignity. His face, presented to us in profile, was gloomy, thoughtful, even philosophic; he might well have been composing a poem. Having finished the sausage, he ordered an Italian salad.

The joke, such as it was, lasted right through our meal. I prolonged it, consciously, as much as I could. So, I think, did Arthur. Tacitly, we helped each other. We were both afraid of a pause. Silence would be too eloquent. And there was so little left for us to talk about. We left the restaurant as soon as was decently possible, accompanied by our attendant, who followed us home, like a nurse, to see us into bed. Through the window of Arthur's room, we watched him take up his former position, under the lamp-post opposite the house.

'How long will he stay there, do you think?' Arthur asked me anxiously.

'The whole night, probably.'

'Oh dear, I do hope not. If he does, I shan't be able to sleep a wink.'

'Perhaps if you appear at your window in pyjamas, he'll go away.'

'Really, William, I hardly think I could do anything so immodest,' Arthur stifled a yawn.

'Well,' I said, a bit awkwardly, 'I think I'll go to bed now.'

'Just what I was going to suggest myself, dear boy.' Holding his chin absently between his finger and thumb, Arthur looked vaguely round the room; added, with a simplicity which excluded all hint of irony:

'We've both had a tiring day.'

Next morning, at any rate, there was no time to feel embarrassed. We had too much to do. No sooner was Arthur's head free from the barber's hands than I came into his room, in my dressing-gown, to hold a conference. The smaller detective in the overcoat was now on duty. Arthur had to admit that he had no idea if either of them had spent the night outside the house. Compassion hadn't after all, disturbed his sleep.

The first problem was, of course, to decide on Arthur's destination. Inquiries must be made at the nearest travel bureau as to possible ships and routes. Arthur had already decided finally against Europe.

'I feel I need a complete change of scene, hard as it is to tear oneself away. One's so confined here, so restricted. As you get older, William, you'll feel that the world gets smaller. The frontiers seem to close in, until there's scarcely room to breathe.'

'What an unpleasant sensation that must be.'

'It is.' Arthur sighed. 'It is indeed. I may be a little over-wrought at the present moment, but I must confess that, to me, the countries of Europe are nothing more or less than a collection of mouse-traps. In some of them, the cheese is of a superior quality, that is the only difference.'

We next discussed which of us should go out and make the inquiries. Arthur was most unwilling to do this.

'But, William, if I go myself, our friend below will most certainly follow me.'

'Of course he will. That's just what we want. As soon as you've let the authorities know that you mean to clear out, you'll have set their minds at rest. I'm sure they ask nothing better than to see your back.'

'Well, you may be right ...'

But Arthur didn't like it. Such tactics revolted all his secretive instincts. 'It seems positively indecent,' he added.

'Look here,' I said, cunningly. 'I'll go if you really want me to. But only on condition that you break the news to Frl. Schroeder yourself while I'm away.'

'Really, dear boy ... No. I couldn't possibly do that. Very well, have it your own way ...'

From my window, half an hour later, I watched him emerge into the street. The detective took, apparently, not the faintest notice of his exit; he was engaged in reading the name-plates within the doorway of the opposite house. Arthur set off briskly, looking neither to left nor right. He reminded me of the man in the poem who fears to catch a glimpse of the demon which is treading in his footsteps. The detective continued to study the name-plates with extreme interest. Then at last, when I had begun to get positively exasperated at his apparent blindness, he straightened himself, pulled out his watch, regarded it with evident surprise, hesitated, appeared to consider, and finally walked away with quick, impatient strides, like a man who has been kept waiting too long. I watched his small figure out of sight in amused admiration. He was an artist.

Meanwhile, I had my own, unpleasant task. I found Frl. Schroeder in the living-room, laying cards, as she did every morning of her life, to discover what would happen during the day. It was no use beating about the bush.

'Frl. Schroeder, Herr Norris has just had some bad news. He'll have to leave Berlin at once. He asked me to tell you ...'

I stopped, feeling horribly uncomfortable, swallowed, blurted out:

'He asked me to tell you that ... he'd like to pay for his room for January and the whole of February as well ...'

Frl. Schroeder was silent. I concluded, lamely—

'Because of his having to go off at such short notice, you see ...'

She didn't look up. There was a muffled sound, and a large tear fell on to the face of a card on the table before her. I felt like crying, too.

'Perhaps ...' I was cowardly. 'It'll only be for a few months. He may be coming back ...'

But Frl. Schroeder either didn't hear or didn't believe this. Her sobs redoubled; she did not attempt to restrain them. Perhaps Arthur's departure was merely the last straw; once started, she had plenty to cry about. The rent and taxes in arrears, the bills she couldn't pay, the rudeness of the coal-man, her pains in the back, her boils, her poverty, her lone-liness, her gradually approaching death. It was dreadful to hear her. I began wandering about the room, nervously touching the furniture, in an ecstasy of discomfort.

'Frl. Schroeder ... it's all right, really, it is ... don't ... please ...'

She got over it at last. Mopping her eyes on a corner of the table-cloth, she deeply sighed. Sadly, her inflamed glance moved over the array of cards. She exclaimed, with a kind of mournful triumph:

'Well, I never! Just look at that, Herr Bradshaw. The ace of spades ... upside down! I might have known something like this would happen. The cards are never wrong.'

Arthur arrived back from the travel bureau in a taxi, about an hour later. His hands were full of papers and illustrated brochures. He seemed tired and depressed.

'How did you get on?' I asked.

'Give me time, William. Give me time ... I'm a little out of breath ...'

Collapsing heavily into a chair, he fanned himself with his hat. I strolled over to the window. The detective wasn't at his usual post. Turning my head to the left, I saw him, however, some way farther down the street, examining the contents of the grocer's shop.

'Is he back already?' Arthur inquired.

I nodded.

'Really? To give the devil his due, that young man will go far in his unsavoury profession ... Do you know, William, he had the effrontery to come right into the office and stand beside me at the counter? I even heard him making in-quiries about a trip to the Harz.'

'Perhaps he really wanted to go there; you never know. He may be having his holidays soon.'

'Well, well ... at all events, it was most upsetting ... I had the greatest difficulty in arriving at the extremely grave decision I had to make.'

'And what's the verdict?'

'I regret to say,' Arthur regarded the buttons on his boot despondently, 'that it will have to be Mexico.'

'Good God!'

'You see, dear boy, the possibilities, at such short notice, are very limited ... I should have greatly preferred Rio, of course, or the Argentine. I even toyed with China. But everywhere, nowadays, there are such absurd formalities. All kinds of stupid and impertinent questions are asked. When I was young, it was very different ... An English gentleman was welcome everywhere, especially with a first-class ticket.'

'And when do you leave?'

'There's a boat at midday tomorrow. I think I shall go to Hamburg today, on the evening train. It's more comfortable, and, perhaps, on the whole, wiser; don't you agree?'

'I dare say. Yes ... This seems a tremendous step to take, all of a sudden. Have you any friends in Mexico?'

Arthur giggled. 'I have friends everywhere, William, or shall I say accomplices?'

'And what shall you do, when you arrive?'

'I shall go straight to Mexico City (a most depressing spot; although I expect it's altered a great deal since I was there in nineteen-eleven). I shall then take rooms in the best hotel and await a moment of inspiration ... I don't suppose I shall starve.'

'No, Arthur,' I laughed, 'I certainly don't see you starving!'

We brightened. We had several drinks. We became quite lively.

Frl. Schroeder was called in, for a start had to be made with Arthur's packing. She was melancholy at first, and inclined to be reproachful, but a glass of cognac worked wonders. She had her own explanation of the reasons for Arthur's sudden departure.

'Ah, Herr Norris, Herr Norris! You should have been more careful. A gentleman at your time of life ought to have experience enough of these things ...' She winked tipsily at me, behind his back. 'Why didn't you stay faithful to your old Schroeder? She would have helped you, she knew about it all the time!'

Arthur, perplexed and vaguely embarrassed, looked questioningly to me for an explanation. I pretended complete ignorance. And now the trunks arrived, fetched down by the porter and his son from the attics at the top of the house. Frl. Schroeder exclaimed, as she packed, over the magnificence of Arthur's clothes. Arthur himself, generous and gay, began distributing largess. The porter got a suit, the porter's wife a bottle of sherry, their son a pair of snakeskin shoes which were much too small for him, but which he insisted he would squeeze into somehow. The piles of newspapers and periodicals were to be sent to a hospital. Arthur certainly gave things away with an air; he knew how to play the Grand Seigneur. The porter's family went away grateful and deeply impressed. I saw that the beginnings of a legend had been created.

As for Frl. Schroeder herself, she was positively loaded with gifts. In addition to the etchings and the Japanese screen, Arthur gave her three flasks of perfume, some hair-lotion, a powder-puff, the entire contents of his wine-cupboard, two beautiful scarves, and, amidst much blushing, a pair of his coveted silk combinations.

'I do wish, William, you'd take something, too. Just some little trifle ...'

'All right, Arthur, thank you very much ... I tell you what, have you still got *Miss Smith's Torture Chamber*? I always liked it the best of those books of yours.'

'You did? Really?' Arthur flushed with pleasure. 'How charming of you to say so! You know, William, I really think I must tell you a secret. The last of my secrets ... I wrote that book myself!'

'Arthur, you didn't!'

'I did, I assure you!' Arthur giggled, delighted. 'Years ago, now ... It's a youthful indiscretion of which I've since felt rather ashamed ... It was printed privately in Paris. I'm told that some of the best-known collectors in Europe have copies in their libraries. It's exceedingly rare.'

'And you never wrote anything else?'

'Never, alas ... I put my genius into my life, not into my art. That remark is not original. Never mind. By the way, since we are on this topic, do you know that I've never said

173

good-bye to my dear Anni? I really think I might ask her to come here this afternoon, don't you? After all, I'm not leaving until after tea.'

'Better not, Arthur. You'll need all your strength for the journey.'

'Well, ha, ha! You may be right. The *pain* of parting would no doubt be most *severe* . . .'

After lunch, Arthur lay down to rest. I took his trunks in a taxi to the Lehrter Station and deposited them in the cloak-room. Arthur was anxious to avoid a lengthy ceremony of departure from the house. The tall detective was on duty now. He watched the loading of the taxi with interest, but made no move to follow.

At tea, Arthur was nervous and depressed. We sat together in the disordered bedroom, with the doors of the empty cupboards standing open and the mattress rolled up at the foot of the bed. I felt apprehensive, for no reason. Arthur rubbed his chin wearily, and sighed:

'I feel like the Old Year, William. I shall soon be gone.'

I smiled. 'A week from now, you'll be sitting on the deck in the sun, while we're still freezing or soaking in this wretched town. I envy you, I can tell you.'

'Do you, dear boy? I sometimes wish I didn't have to do so much travelling. Mine is essentially a domestic nature. I ask nothing better than to settle down.'

'Well, why don't you, then?'

'That's what I so often ask myself . . . Something always seems to prevent it.'

At last it was time to go.

With infinite fuss, Arthur put on his coat, lost and found his gloves, gave a last touch to his wig. I picked up his suitcase and we went out into the hall. Nothing was left but the worst, the ordeal of saying good-bye to Frl. Schroeder. She emerged from the living-room, moist-eyed.

'Well, Herr Norris . . .'

The door-bell rang loudly, and there was a double knock on the door. The interruption made Arthur jump.

'Good gracious! Whoever can that be?'

'It's the postman, I expect,' said Frl. Schroeder. 'Excuse me, Herr Bradshaw ...'

Barely had she opened the door when the man outside it pushed past her into the hall. It was Schmidt.

That he was drunk was obvious, even before he opened his mouth. He stood swaying uncertainly, hatless, his tie over one shoulder, his collar awry. His huge face was inflamed and swollen so that his eyes were mere slits. The hall was a small place for four people. We were standing so close together that I could smell his breath. It stank vilely.

Arthur, at my side, uttered an incoherent sound of dismay, and I myself could only gape. Strange as it may seem, I was entirely unprepared for this apparition. During the last twenty-four hours, I had forgotten Schmidt's existence altogether.

He was the master of the situation, and he knew it. His face fairly beamed with malice. Kicking the front door shut behind him with his foot, he surveyed the two of us; Arthur's coat, the suitcase in my hand.

'Doing a bunk, eh?' He spoke loudly, as if addressing a large audience in the middle distance. 'I see ... thought you'd give me the slip, did you?' He advanced a pace; he confronted the trembling and dismayed Arthur. 'Lucky I came, wasn't it? Unlucky for you ...'

Arthur emitted another sound, this time a kind of squeak of terror. It seemed to excite Schmidt to a positive frenzy of rage. He clenched his fists, he shouted with astonishing violence:

'You dirty tyke!'

He raised his arm. He may actually have been going to strike Arthur; if so, I shouldn't have had time to prevent it. All I could do, within the instant, was to drop the suitcase to the ground. But Frl. Schroeder's reactions were quicker and more effective. She hadn't the ghost of an idea what the fuss was all about. That didn't worry her. Enough that Herr Norris was being insulted by an unknown, drunken man. With a shrill battle-cry of indignation, she charged. Her outstretched palms caught Schmidt in the small of the back, propelled him forwards, like an engine shunting trucks. Unsteady on his feet and taken completely by surprise, he blundered headlong through the open doorway into the living-room and fell sprawling, face downwards, on the carpet. Frl. Schroeder promptly turned the key in the lock. The whole manœuvre was the work of about five seconds.

'Such cheek!' exclaimed Frl. Schroeder. Her cheeks were bright red with the exertion. 'He comes barging in here as if the place belonged to him. And intoxicated ... *pfui!* ... the disgusting pig!'

She seemed to find nothing particularly mysterious in the incident. Perhaps she connected Schmidt somehow with Margot and the ill-fated baby. If so, she was too tactful to say so. A tremendous rattle of knocks on the living-room door excused me from any attempt at inventing explanations.

'Won't he be able to get out at the back?' Arthur inquired nervously.

'You can set your mind at rest, Herr Norris. The kitchen door's locked.' Frl. Schroeder turned menacingly upon the invisible Schmidt. 'Be quiet, you scoundrel! I'll attend to you in a minute!'

'All the same ...' Arthur was on pins and needles, 'I think we ought to be going ...'

'How are you going to get rid of him?' I asked Frl. Schroeder.

'Oh, don't you worry about that, Herr Bradshaw. As soon as you're gone, I'll get the porter's son up. He'll go quietly enough, I promise you. If he doesn't, he'll be sorry ...'

We said good-bye hurriedly. Frl. Schroeder was too excited and triumphant to be emotional. Arthur kissed her on both cheeks. She stood waving to us from the top of the stairs. A fresh outburst of muffled knocking was audible behind her.

We were in the taxi, and half-way to the station before Arthur recovered his composure sufficiently to be able to talk.

'Dear me ... I've seldom made such an exceedingly unpleasant exit from any town, I think ...'

'What you might call a rousing send-off.' I glanced behind me to make sure that the other taxi, with the tall detective, was still following us.

'What do you think he'll do, William? Perhaps he'll go straight to the police?'

'I'm pretty sure he won't. As long as he's drunk, they won't listen to him, and by the time he's sober, he'll see himself that it's no good. He hasn't the least idea where you're going, either. For all he knows, you'll be out of the country tonight.'

'You may be right, dear boy. I hope so, I'm sure. I must say I hate to leave you exposed to his malice. You will be most careful, won't you?'

'Oh, Schmidt won't bother me. I'm not worth it, from his point of view. He'll probably find another victim easily enough. I dare say he's got plenty on his books.'

'While he was in my employ he certainly had opportunities,' Arthur agreed thoughtfully. 'And I've no doubt he made full use of them. The creature had talents – of a perverted kind ... Oh, unquestionably ... yes ...'

At length it was all over. The misunderstanding with the cloak-room official, the fuss about the luggage, the finding of a corner seat, the giving of the tip. Arthur leant out of the carriage window; I stood on the platform. We had five minutes to spare.

'You'll remember me to Otto, won't you?'

'I will.'

'And give my love to Anni?'

'Of course.'

'I wish they could have been here.'

'It's a pity, isn't it?'

'But it would have been unwise, under the circumstances. Don't you agree?'

'Yes.'

I longed for the train to start. There was nothing more to say, it seemed, except the things which must never be said now because it was too late. Arthur seemed aware of the vacuum. He groped about uneasily in his stock of phrases.

'I wish you were coming with me, William ... I shall miss you terribly, you know.'

'Shall you?' I smiled awkwardly, feeling exquisitely uncomfortable.

'I shall, indeed ... You've always been such a support to me. From the first moment we met ...'

I blushed. It was astonishing what a cad he could make me feel. Hadn't I, after all, misunderstood him? Hadn't I misjudged him? Hadn't I, in some obscure way, behaved very badly? To change the subject, I asked:

'You remember that journey? I simply couldn't understand why they made such a fuss at the frontier. I suppose they'd got their eye on you already?'

Arthur didn't care much for this reminiscence.

'I suppose they had ... Yes.'

Another silence. I glanced at the clock, despairingly. One more minute to go. Fumblingly, he began again.

'Try not to think too hardly of me, William ... I should hate that ...'

'What nonsense, Arthur ...' I did my best to pass it off lightly. 'How absurd you are!'

'This life is so very complex. If my behaviour hasn't always been quite consistent, I can truly say that I am and always shall be loyal to the Party, at heart ... Say you believe that, please?'

He was outrageous, grotesque, entirely without shame. But what was I to answer? At that moment, had he demanded it, I'd have sworn that two and two make five.

'Yes, Arthur, I do believe it.'

'Thank you, William ... Oh dear, now we really are off. I do hope all my trunks are in the van. God bless you, dear boy. I shall think of you always. Where's my mackintosh. Ah, that's all right. Is my hat on straight? Good-bye. Write often, won't you. Good-bye.'

'Good-bye, Arthur.'

The train, gathering speed, drew his manicured hand from mine. I walked a little way down the platform and stood waving until the last coach was out of sight.

As I turned to leave the station, I nearly collided with a man who had been standing just behind me. It was the detective.

'Excuse me, *Herr Kommissar*,' I murmured.

But he did not even smile.

CHAPTER SIXTEEN

Early in March, after the elections, it turned suddenly mild and warm. 'Hitler's weather,' said the porter's wife; and her son remarked jokingly that we ought to be grateful to van der Lubbe, because the burning of the Reichstag had melted the snow. 'Such a nice-looking boy,' observed Frl. Schroeder, with a sigh. 'However could he go and do a dreadful thing like that?' The porter's wife snorted.

Our street looked quite gay when you turned into it and saw the black-white-red flags hanging motionless from windows against the blue spring sky. On the Nollendorfplatz people were sitting out of doors before the café in their overcoats, reading about the *coup d'état* in Bavaria. Göring spoke from the radio horn at the corner. Germany is awake, he said. An ice-cream shop was open. Uniformed Nazis strode hither and thither, with serious, set faces, as though on weighty errands. The newspaper readers by the café turned their heads to watch them pass and smiled and seemed pleased.

They smiled approvingly at these youngsters in their big, swaggering boots who were going to upset the Treaty of Versailles. They were pleased because it would soon be summer, because Hitler had promised to protect the small tradesmen, because their newspapers told them that the good times were coming. They were suddenly proud of being blonde. And they thrilled with a furtive, sensual pleasure, like schoolboys, because the Jews, their business rivals, and the Marxists, a vaguely defined minority of people who didn't concern them, had been satisfactorily found guilty of the defeat and the inflation, and were going to catch it.

The town was full of whispers. They told of illegal midnight arrests, of prisoners tortured in the S.A. barracks, made to spit on Lenin's picture, swallow castor-oil, eat old socks. They were drowned by the loud, angry voice of the Government, contradicting through its thousand mouths. But not even Göring could silence Helen Pratt. She had decided to investigate the atrocities on her own account. Morning, noon and night, she nosed round the city, ferreting out the victims or their relations, cross-examining them for details. These unfortunate people were reticent, of course, and deadly scared. They didn't want a second dose. But Helen was as relentless as their torturers. She bribed, cajoled, pestered. Sometimes, losing her patience, she threatened. What would happen to them afterwards frankly didn't interest her. She was out to get facts.

It was Helen who first told me that Bayer was dead. She had absolutely reliable evidence. One of the office staff, since released, had seen his corpse in the Spandau barracks. 'It's a funny thing,' she added, 'his left ear was torn right off ... God knows why. It's my belief that some of this gang are simply looneys. Why, Bill, what's the matter? You're going green round the gills.'

'That's how I feel,' I said.

An awkward thing had happened to Fritz Wendel. A few days before, he had had a motor accident; he had sprained his wrist and scratched the skin off his cheek. The injuries weren't at all serious, but he had to wear a big piece of sticking-plaster and carry his arm in a sling. And now, in spite of the lovely weather, he wouldn't venture out of doors. Bandages of any kind gave rise to misunderstandings, especially when, like Fritz, you had a dark complexion and coal-black hair. Passers-by made unpleasant and threatening remarks. Fritz wouldn't admit this, of course. 'Hell, what I mean, one feels such a darn' fool.' He had become exceedingly cautious. He wouldn't refer to politics at all, even when we were alone together. 'Eventually it had to happen,' was his only comment on the new régime. As he said this, he avoided my eyes.

The whole city lay under an epidemic of discreet, infectious fear. I could feel it, like influenza, in my bones. When the first news of the house-searchings began to come in, I had consulted with Frl. Schroeder about the papers which Bayer had given me. We hid them and my copy of the

Communist Manifesto under the wood-pile in the kitchen. Un-building and rebuilding the wood-pile took half an hour, and before it was finished our precautions had begun to seem rather childish. I felt a bit ashamed of myself, and consequently exaggerated the importance and danger of my position to Frl. Schroeder, who listened respectfully, with rising indignation. 'You mean to say they'd come into *my* flat, Herr Bradshaw? Well, of all the cheek. But just let them try it! Why, I'd box their ears for them; I declare I would!'

A night or two after this, I was woken by a tremendous banging on the outside door. I sat up in bed and switched on the light. It was just three o'clock. Now I'm for it, I thought. I wondered if they'd allow me to ring up the Embassy. Smooth-ing my hair tidy with my hand, I tried, not very successfully, to assume an expression of haughty contempt. But when, at last, Frl. Schroeder had shuffled out to see what was the matter, it was only a lodger from next door who'd come to the wrong flat because he was drunk.

After this scare, I suffered from sleeplessness. I kept fancy-ing I heard heavy wagons drawing up outside our house. I lay waiting in the dark for the ringing of the door-bell. A minute. Five minutes. Ten. One morning, as I stared, half asleep, at the wallpaper above my bed, the pattern suddenly formed itself into a chain of little hooked crosses. What was worse, I noticed that everything in the room was really a kind of brown: either green-brown, black-brown, yellow-brown, or red-brown; but all brown, unmistakably. When I had had breakfast and taken a purgative, I felt better.

One morning, I had a visit from Otto.

It must have been about half-past six when he rang our bell. Frl. Schroeder wasn't up yet; I let him in myself. He was in a filthy state, his hair tousled and matted, a stain of dirty blood down the side of his face from a scratch on the temples.

'*Servus, Willi,*' he muttered. He put out his hand suddenly and clutched my arm. With difficulty, I saved him from falling. But he wasn't drunk, as I at first imagined; simply exhausted. He flopped down into a chair in my room. When I returned from shutting the outside door, he was already asleep.

It was rather a problem to know what to do with him. I had a pupil coming early. Finally, Frl. Schroeder and I managed, between us, to lug him, still half asleep, into Arthur's old bedroom and lay him on the bed. He was incredibly heavy. No sooner was he laid on his back than he began to snore. His snores were so loud that you could hear them in my room, even when the door was shut; they continued, audibly, throughout the lesson. Meanwhile, my pupil, a very nice young man who hoped soon to become a schoolmaster, was eagerly adjuring me not to believe the stories, 'invented by Jewish emigrants,' about the political persecution.

'Actually,' he assured me, 'these so-called communists are merely a handful of criminals, the scum of the streets. And most of them are not Germans at all.'

'I thought,' I said politely, 'that you were telling me just now that they drew up the Weimar Constitution?'

This rather staggered him for the moment; but he made a good recovery.

'No, pardon me, the Weimar Constitution was the work of Marxist Jews.'

'Ah, the Jews ... to be sure.'

My pupil smiled. My stupidity made him feel a bit superior. I think he even liked me for it. A particularly loud snore came from the next room.

'For a foreigner,' he politely conceded, 'German politics are very complicated.'

'Very,' I agreed.

Otto woke about tea-time, ravenously hungry. I went out and bought sausages and eggs and Frl. Schroeder cooked him a meal while he washed. Afterwards we sat together in my room. Otto smoked one cigarette after another; he was very nervy and couldn't sit still. His clothes were getting ragged and the collar of his sweater was frayed. His face was full of hollows. He looked like a grown man now, at least five years older.

Frl. Schroeder made him take off his jacket. She mended it while we talked, interjecting, at intervals: 'Is it possible? The idea ... how dare they do such a thing? That's what I'd like to know?'

Otto had been on the run for a fortnight, now, he told us. Two nights after the Reichstag fire, his old enemy, Werner Baldow, had come round, with six others of his storm-troop, to 'arrest' him. Otto used the word without irony; he seemed to find it quite natural. 'There's lots of old scores being paid off nowadays,' he added, simply.

Nevertheless, Otto had escaped, through a skylight, after kicking one of the Nazis in the face. They had shot at him twice, but missed. Since then he'd been wandering about Berlin, sleeping only in the daytime, walking the streets at night, for fear of house-raids. The first week hadn't been so bad; comrades had put him up, one passing him on to another. But that was getting too risky now. So many of them were dead or in concentration camps. He'd been sleeping when he could, taking short naps on benches in parks. But he could never rest properly. He had always to be on the watch. He couldn't stick it any longer. Tomorrow he was going to leave Berlin. He'd try to work his way down to the Saar. Somebody had told him that was the easiest frontier to cross. It was dangerous, of course, but better than being cooped up here.

I asked what had become of Anni. Otto didn't know. He'd heard she was with Werner Baldow again. What else could you expect? He wasn't even bitter; he just didn't care. And Olga? Oh, Olga was doing finely. That remarkable business woman had escaped the clean-up through the influence of one of her customers, an important Nazi official. Others had begun to go there, now. Her future was assured.

Otto had heard about Bayer.

'They say Thälmann's dead, too. And Renn. *Junge, Junge …*'

We exchanged rumours about other well-known names. Frl. Schroeder shook her head and murmured over each. She was so genuinely upset that nobody would have dreamed she was hearing most of them for the first time in her life.

The talk turned naturally to Arthur. We showed Otto the postcards of Tampico which had arrived, for both of us, only a week ago. He examined them with admiration.

'I suppose he's carrying on the work there?'

'What work?'

'The Party work, of course!'

'Oh, yes,' I hastily agreed. 'Of course he is.'

'It was a bit of luck that he went away when he did, wasn't it?'

'Yes ... it certainly was.'

Otto's eyes shone.

'We needed more men like old Arthur in the Party. He was a speaker, if you like!'

His enthusiasm warmed Frl. Schroeder's heart. The tears stood in her eyes.

'I always shall say Herr Norris was one of the best and finest and straightest gentlemen I ever knew.'

We were all silent. In the twilit room we dedicated a grateful, reverent moment to Arthur's memory. Then Otto continued in a tone of profound conviction:

'Do you know what I think? He's working for us out there, making propaganda and raising money; and one day, you'll see, he'll come back. Hitler and the rest of them will have to look out for themselves then ...'

It was getting dark outside. Frl. Schroeder rose to turn on the light. Otto said he must be going. He'd decided to make a start this evening now that he was feeling rested. By daybreak, he'd be clear of Berlin altogether. Frl. Schroeder protested vigorously. She had taken a great fancy to him.

'Nonsense, Herr Otto. You'll sleep here tonight. You need a thorough rest. Those Nazis will never find you here. They'd have to cut me into little pieces first.'

Otto smiled and thanked her warmly, but he wasn't to be persuaded. We had to let him go. Frl. Schroeder filled his pockets with sandwiches. I gave him three handkerchiefs, an old penknive, and a map of Germany printed on a postcard which had been slipped in through our letter-box to advertise a firm of bicycle makers. Even this could be better than nothing, for Otto's geography was alarmingly weak. Unguided, he would probably have found himself heading for Poland. I wanted to give him some money, too. At first he wouldn't hear of it, and I had to resort to the disingenuous argument that we were brother communists. 'Besides,' I added craftily, 'you

184

can pay me back.' We shook hands solemnly on this.

He was astonishingly cheerful at parting. From his manner you would have supposed that it was we who needed encouragement, not he.

'Cheer up, Willi. Don't you worry ... Our time will come.'

'Of course it will. Good-bye, Otto. Good luck.'

'Good-bye.'

We watched him set off, from my window. Frl. Schroeder had begun to sniff.

'Poor boy ... Do you think he's got a chance, Herr Bradshaw? I declare I shan't sleep the whole night, thinking about him. It's as if he were my own son.'

Otto turned once to look back; he waved his hand jauntily and smiled. Then he thrust his hands into his pockets, hunched his shoulders and strode rapidly away, with the heavy, agile gait of a boxer, down the long dark street and into the lighted square, to be lost amidst the sauntering crowds of his enemies.

I never saw or heard of him again.

Three weeks later I returned to England.

I had been in London nearly a month, when Helen Pratt came round to see me. She had arrived back from Berlin the day before, having triumphantly succeeded, with a series of scalding articles, in getting the sale of her periodical forbidden throughout Germany. Already she'd been offered a much better job in America. She was sailing within a fortnight to attack New York.

She exuded vitality, success and news. The Nazi Revolution had positively given her a new lease of life. To hear her talk, you might have thought she had spent the last two months hiding in Dr Goebbels' writing-desk or under Hitler's bed. She had the details of every private conversation and the lowdown on every scandal. She knew what Schacht had said to Norman, what von Papen had said to Meissner, what Schleicher might shortly be expected to say to the Crown Prince. She knew the amounts of Thyssen's cheques. She had new stories about Roehm, about Heines, about Göring and his uniforms. 'My God, Bill, what a racket!' She talked for hours.

Exhausted at last of all the misdeeds of the great, she started on the lesser fry.

'I suppose you heard all about Pregnitz affair, didn't you?'

'No. Not a word.'

'Gosh, you are behind the times!' Helen brightened at the prospect of yet another story. 'Why, that can't have been more than a week after you left. They kept it fairly quiet, of course, in the papers. A pal of mine on the *New York Herald* gave me all the dope.'

But, on this occasion, the dope wasn't all on Helen's side. Naturally, she didn't know everything about van Hoorn. The temptation to fill out the gaps in her story, or, at least, to betray my knowledge of them, was considerable. Thank goodness, I didn't yield to it. She was no more to be trusted with news than a cat with a saucer of milk. And, indeed, I was astonished how much her resourceful colleague had found out on his own account.

The police must have been keeping Kuno under observation ever since our Swiss visit. Their patience had certainly been remarkable, bcause, for three whole months, he had done absolutely nothing to arouse their suspicions. Then, quite suddenly, at the beginning of April, he had got into communication with Paris. He was ready, he said, to reconsider the business they had discussed. His first letter was short and carefully vague; a week later, under pressure from van Hoorn, he wrote a much longer one, giving explicit details of what he proposed to sell. He sent it by special messenger, taking all due precautions and employing a code. Within a few hours, the police had deciphered every word.

They went round to arrest him that afternoon at his flat. Kuno was out, having tea with a friend. His manservant had just time to telephone to him a guarded warning, before the detectives took possession. Kuno seems to have lost his head completely. He did the worst thing possible; jumped into a taxi and drove straight to the Zoo Station. The plain-clothes men there recognized him at once. They'd been supplied with his description that very morning, and who could mistake Kuno? Cruelly enough, they let him buy a ticket for the next available train; it happened to be going to Frankfurt-on-the-

Oder. As he went up the steps to the platform, two detectives came forward to arrest him; but he was ready for that, and bolted down again. The exits were all guarded, of course. Kuno's pursuers lost him in the crowd; caught sight of him again as he ran through the swing doors into the lavatory. By the time they had elbowed their way through the people, he had already locked himself into one of the closets. ('The newspapers,' said Helen, scornfully, 'called it a telephone-box.') The detectives ordered him to come out. He wouldn't answer. Finally, they had to clear the whole place and get ready to break down the door. It was then that Kuno shot himself.

'And he couldn't even make a decent job of that,' Helen added. 'Fired crooked. Nearly blew his eye out; bled like a pig. They had to take him to hospital to finish him off.'

'Poor devil.'

Helen looked at me curiously.

'Good riddance to bad rubbish, *I* should have said.'

'You see,' I apologetically confessed, 'I knew him, slightly ...'

'Well, I'm blowed! Did you? Sorry. I must say, Bill, you're a nice little chap, but you do have some queer friends. Well, this ought to interest you, then. You knew Pregnitz was a fairy, of course?'

'I rather guessed something of the kind.'

'Well, my pal got on to the inside story of why Pregnitz went in for this treason racket at all. He needed cash quickly, you see, because he was being blackmailed. And who, do you think, was doing the blackmailing? None other than the secretary of another dear old friend of yours, Harris.'

'Norris?'

'That's right. Well, it seems that this precious secretary ... what was *his* name, by the way?'

'Schmidt.'

'Was it? I dare say. Just suits him ... Schmidt had got hold of a lot of letters Pregnitz had written to some youth. God alone knows how. Pretty hot stuff they must have been, if Pregnitz was prepared to risk his skin to pay for them. Shouldn't have thought it was worth it myself. Rather face the music. But these people never have any guts ...'

'Did your friend find out what happened to Schmidt afterwards?' I asked.

'Don't suppose so, no. Why should he? What *does* happen to these creatures? He's probably abroad, somewhere, blowing the cash. He'd got quite a lot out of Pregnitz, already, it seems. As far as I'm concerned, he's welcome to it. Who cares?'

'I know one person,' I said, 'who might be interested.'

A few days after this, I got a letter from Arthur. He was in Mexico City now, and hating it.

Let me advise you, my dear boy, with all the solemnity of which I am capable, *never* to set foot in this odious town. On the material plane, it is true, I manage to provide myself with most of my accustomed comforts. But the complete lack of intelligent society, at least, as *I* understand the term, afflicts me deeply ...

Arthur didn't say much about his business affairs; he was more guarded than of old.

'Times are very bad, but, on the whole, I can't complain,' was his only admission. On the subject of Germany, he let himself go, however:

It makes me positively *tremble* with indignation to think of the workers delivered over to these men, who, whatever you may say, are nothing more or less than *criminals*.

And, a little farther down the page:

It is indeed tragic to see how, even in these days, a *clever unscrupulous liar* can deceive millions.

In conclusion, he paid a handsome tribute to Bayer:

A man I always admired and respected. I feel proud to be able to say that I was his friend.

I next heard of Arthur in June, on a postcard from California.

I am basking here in the sunshine of Santa Monica. After Mexico, this is indeed a Paradise. I have a little venture on foot, not unconnected with the film industry. I think and hope it may turn out quite profitably. Will write again soon.

He did write, and sooner, no doubt, than he had originally intended. By the next mail, I got another postcard, dated a day later.

The very worst has happened. Am leaving for Costa Rica tonight. All details from there.

This time I got a short letter.

If Mexico was *Purgatory*, this is the *Inferno* itself.
My Californian idyll was rudely cut short by the appearance of SCHMIDT!!! The creature's ingenuity is positively *superhuman*. Not only had he followed me there, but he had succeeded in finding out the exact nature of the little deal I was hoping to put through. I was entirely at his mercy. I was compelled to give him most of my hard-earned savings and depart at once.
Just imagine, he even had the insolence to suggest that I should *employ* him, as before!!
I don't know yet whether I have suceeded in throwing him off my track. I hardly *dare* to hope.

At least, Arthur wasn't left long in doubt. A postcard soon followed the letter.

The MONSTER has arrived!!! May try Peru.

Other glimpses of this queer journey reached me from time to time. Arthur had no luck in Lima. Schmidt turned up within the week. From there, the chase proceeded to Chile.

'An attempt to *exterminate* the reptile failed miserably,' he wrote from Valparaiso. 'I succeeded only in arousing its venom.'

I suppose this is Arthur's ornate way of saying that he had tried to get Schmidt murdered.

In Valparaiso, a truce seems, however, to have been at last declared. For the next postcard, announcing a train journey to to the Argentine, indicates a new state of affairs.

    We leave this afternoon, *together*, for Buenos Aires. Am too depressed to write more now.

At present, they are in Rio. Or were when I last heard. It is impossible to predict their movements. Any day Schmidt may set off for fresh hunting-grounds, dragging Arthur after him, a protesting employer-prisoner. Their new partnership won't be so easy to dissolve as their old one. Henceforward, they are doomed to walk the Earth together. I often think about them and wonder what I should do if, by any unlucky chance, we were to meet. I am not particularly sorry for Arthur. After all, he no doubt gets his hands on a good deal of money. But he is very sorry for himself.

'Tell me, William,' his last letter concluded, '*what* have I done to deserve all this?'

All these books are available at your local bookshop or newsagent, or can be ordered direct from the publisher.

To order direct from the publisher just tick the titles you want and fill in the form below.

Name _____

Address _____

_____

Send to:
Panther Cash Sales
PO Box 11, Falmouth, Cornwall TR10 9EN.

Please enclose remittance to the value of the cover price plus:

UK 45p for the first book, 20p for the second book plus 14p per copy for each additional book ordered to a maximum charge of £1.63.

BFPO and Eire 45p for the first book, 20p for the second book plus 14p per copy for the next 7 books, thereafter 8p per book.

Overseas 75p for the first book and 21p for each additional book.

Panther Books reserve the right to show new retail prices on covers, which may differ from those previously advertised in the text or elsewhere.